W9-BVS-712

LAST
NIGHT
AT THE
CIRCLE
CINEMA

LAST NIGHT AT THE CIRCLE CINEMA

Emily Franklin

carolrhoda LAB

MINNEAPOLIS

Carolrhoda Lab™ is a trademark of Lerner Publishing Group, Inc.

Carolrhoda Lab™
An imprint of Carolrhoda Books
A division of Lerner Publishing Group, Inc.
241 First Avenue North
Minneapolis, MN 55401 USA

For reading levels and more information, look up this title at www.lernerbooks.com.

The images in this book are used with the permission of: © iStockphoto.com/
Gordan1 (film frame); © Kolett/Moment Open/Getty Images (equation); © Todd
Strand/Independent Picture Service (baseball); © PhotoDisc Royalty Free by Getty
Images (pocket watch); © iStockphoto.com/dehooks (pizza); © iStockphoto.com/
PeterAustin (hammer); © Laura Westlund/Independent Picture Service (cat box
illustration and guitar chord illustration).

Main body text set in Janson Text LT Std 10.5/15.
Typeface provided by Linotype AG.

Library of Congress Cataloging-in-Publication Data

The Cataloging-in-Publication Data for *Last Night at the Circle Cinema* is on file at
the Library of Congress.
ISBN 978-1-4677-7489-5 (lib. bdg.)
ISBN 978-1-4677-8815-1 (EB pdf)

Manufactured in the United States of America
1 – BP – 7/15/15

This book is for Sam

Livvy

I'm not going to lie. If there's one thing I get in trouble for, it's being too honest. Like I'd just tell someone that they don't have the strongest backhand (since they asked), or when Marta wanted to know if I thought she could pull off wearing a blue feather clipped in her hair even though she's not Native American or on TV, I just looked right at her and said, nope.

Which was why it was so bizarre that I couldn't even begin to admit to Codman that I liked him. That I had liked him for over a year since drama elective when we had to improvise buying something at a grocery store and Codman chose two big melons (which I have—just saying for the record). I liked him when he played old records for me in the space he converted from a closet into a listening room, and I liked him when he read the short stories I wrote for the *Growing Tree*, our award-winning but poorly named school literary magazine. I liked him six months ago when we first agreed to meet outside the movie theater the night before graduation, the last night of our senior year, the "ultimate night signifying the end of our youth," as I had written in a story and which Codman had crossed out with the stub of a pencil he always kept in his pocket. "What can I say?" He'd raised his eyebrows and licked the tip of the pencil. "I like to edit."

He was editing now, licking the rain from his lips as though every droplet had a secret that he wasn't spilling. Had he written a speech for graduation? Probably not. And if he had, he hadn't asked me to read it.

"Are you waiting to actually drown or what?" Codman asked now. Water droplets clung to his earlobes until they couldn't hold their own weight and joined the puddles that formed around us.

"It's not my fault Bertucci's not here," I said, even though I kind of thought it might be. "So, you got the e-mail too?" Bertucci's letter had popped up in my inbox first thing in the morning, and it freaked me out seeing it there—he wasn't much of an e-mailer, and I wasn't much of a break-the-rules person.

"What e-mail?" Codman asked. I didn't want to soak my phone to show Codman the note, so I started to describe it, but he interrupted me. "E-mail? What about the yearbook thing?"

"What yearbook thing?" I sighed—together for the first time in weeks and already unable to communicate. What e-mail, what yearbook, what anything?

The truth was that the yearbook depressed me. All those times-gone-by photos—last time we'll sprawl on the fall grass with our heads on backpacks, last Senior Fling, last look at the people whose names would slip away from us in just a few years, last class photo. Last everything.

So while I owned a *Brookville Baton*, it was in a box of crap in my room as though I'd begun packing for college. The e-mail was portable, though, and I'd printed out

Bertucci's odd invitation to the Circle insisting the three of us spend the night, folded it, and stuck it in my back pocket like I needed it as evidence.

"Never mind," Codman said, clearing his throat like he didn't want to go into why we were standing there.

I shook the plastic bag in my hand. Inside were rain boots I should have been wearing and Bertucci's ragged sweater he'd bequeathed to me the night I thought he'd finally admit his feelings for me.

"My shoes are basically fucked," Codman said, but he wasn't looking down at his shoes. He opened his mouth up like he was intent on drinking the polluted rain. His shirt was buttoned incorrectly, like he got dressed with his eyes closed, and he noticed me noticing but didn't fix it.

Codman had this impenetrable quality that made him look supremely comfortable all the time. Like when Benny Freeman spontaneously kissed him on the cheek, and he didn't flinch. Even though everyone knew Benny had a thing for guys and Codman didn't, Codman just went with it.

"I know just where to get you another pair," I said and touched his tennis shoe with my clog and then regretted it.

He looked the same as a few weeks before, the last time we'd really hung out, but my touch was too familiar. I looked more closely; he didn't look the same. Neither of us did.

"I don't know why we're even waiting."

"He said ten o'clock," I reminded Codman. I felt we had to do everything Bertucci had outlined. It was the ultimate test of our friendship, the summary of everything we'd been through together.

"Well, it doesn't matter," he said. "Three more minutes, and then I say we head in." He looked at his wrist out of habit. His watch had broken months ago, and he hadn't replaced it, sort of figuring his dad might give him one for a graduation gift. I kind of hoped he didn't; I liked watching

3

Codman look at his wrist and the surprise that slid over his face each time he remembered there was nothing there.

"I hate going in without him."

Yeah, I'd have been lying if I said I wasn't tempted to follow Codman just about anywhere—especially someplace dark, deserted, and filled with free candy—but the idea had sprouted from the mass of weirdness that was Bertucci's brain; it was his plan, and I felt it wasn't right to start off without him.

Bertucci was the first to find out the Circle was closing. He always knew things before anyone else. "Forty-two years of business boarded up just like that," he's said as though it was his place of employment or his family's. Like it meant everything.

And it did mean something. All those matinees as a kid; my twelfth birthday when Kyla Bernhard threw up on my lap after eating too many Jujubes; the first time Jake Leftkowitz ever felt me up; all those nights Codman, Bertucci, and I would hang around outside debating which movie to see, sometimes talking so long we wound up seeing nothing, which I kind of thought was maybe the point.

Bertucci wanted us to meet here as a final farewell, the kind of night we'd look back on and remember in detail.

Codman licked his lips. "Look, waiting in the rain is pointless. He'd want us to go in, don't you think?"

I shrugged. Bertucci had a habit of being late, of wanting to arrive after the action started, to figure out where to place himself.

Codman's eyes were this super-intense shade of green, especially in the leftover streetlight, and he narrowed them like a cat. He looked evil—in a hot sort of way. He could do that—look two things at once. Like with the shoes. I was with him when he bought those shoes. He knew he wanted a very particular kind of indoor soccer shoe and where he could get them but insisted we look around at a bunch of other places first. The second store was Ski 'n' Golf. They sell only ski and golf stuff. This is printed on their sign, in their ads, and so on. But of course Codman went in there with a totally straight face and said, "Hi!" and proceeded to ask for soccer shoes. "We only sell items relating to skiing and golf." "Oh, so you don't have any indoor soccer shoes?" "No, sorry." Codman held up a golf shoe. "Now, see, this is almost perfect. But without the spikes. Got anything like that?" If anyone else tried it they'd get kicked out or slapped. But Codman never gets called out for it, because he's so wide-eyed. Innocent while being kind of a dick.

I felt for my phone in my pocket, my thumbs ready to swipe 'n' type without even looking. It felt good, just saying stuff to him, sending my thoughts off into space. *Waiting 4 U.* I hit send before Codman saw.

"Anyway, Bertucci'd probably show up with a hitchhiker he picked up on Route 9," I muttered. Bertucci wouldn't have done either of those things because, of any of us, he was the kindest. A knight in a post-punk kind of way. "Okay, it's officially pouring."

The sky was so thick with rain and clouds, you couldn't see anything specific, just a mass of water, the odd burst of lightning. A lull between thunder rumbles made for a peaceful moment. Codman and I stood there saying nothing, not touching. It was sort of cool. And sort of pathetic. Possibly it was romantic, if I had had any idea what he felt or was able to admit how much I wanted to feel his wet hand wrap around mine.

For us to talk about what was happening under the surface.

Another round of thunder made me jump. I could make out Bertucci's face in the darkness. "It was a dark and stormy night!" Bertucci always appreciated clichés.

I could feel Bertucci pause right before he hugged me,

his pale gray eyes checking in with me as though he wanted to make sure it was okay. I always found it both sweet that he checked and lame, like if he just did it he wouldn't kill the thrill, and maybe I would have found him more appealing. But then I felt guilty for feeling that. I've been accused of overanalyzing everything, so maybe the pause meant nothing.

I started shivering, both because his arrival surprised me and because the weather had gotten to me. It was supposed to be warm out, and maybe it would have been, but the rain tamped down any heat. Plus it had been a cold spring anyway, the kind where you went out without a coat or sweatshirt and then cursed yourself because you were fooled again by the ineffectual sunlight. The kind where I'd watched from Codman's listening room while he and Bertucci had chucked a Frisbee back and forth, not wanting to join in because I was too cold and didn't want to borrow Codman's sweatshirt because then he'd have known how I felt.

Plus, I wanted to overanalyze the song he'd put on for me on the record player. It was called "Girls Talk," and I'd never heard it before. It was one of those songs Betucci liked best—it sounded happy but was littered with words like *murder, pretending, living end.* I'd listened to the lyrics, carefully picked up the needle and placed it back at the beginning, all the while watching the Frisbee sail from Bertucci's hands to Codman's. Their mouths were moving, but I had no idea what they were saying.

• • • •

Outside the Circle Cinema, I remembered Bertucci's crumpled cotton sweater. I slid it on fast before it got too wet. The maroon cotton hung past my waist and over my hands. Bertucci was tall but too awkward to be recruited for basketball, but so ridiculously smart that he'd won the Gleason Physics Scholarship to UC–Berkeley. The sweater provided instant relief from my shaking. Bertucci was always doing that, thinking of what you needed. Sometimes even before you'd thought of it yourself. Giving you the shirt off his back.

"Hey, Bertucci," I whispered and pretended to thwack him with one of the too-long sleeves.

"Livvy," he said. He was the only one who called me that except for my grandpa who died. And probably if anyone else tried to use that name I'd have corrected them.

But with Bertucci it was okay.

I had met him before I met Codman, but he and Codman were already friends since before me. Since they both referred to each other by their last names, I followed suit, even though I had never pictured myself as one of those girls who used last names like she was trying to be one of the guys. It just sort of happened.

Plus, everyone called Bertucci Bertucci. They gave him shirts and placemats and advertising posters from that chain pizza place even though it had absolutely zero to do with him and his family. When a franchise opened near school, Bertucci just shook his head. Codman said "Fuck" for him, because that's what he felt. Bertucci didn't even enjoy Italian food. He hated tomatoes and he was allergic to gluten, both of which were in practically everything on the menu.

Lightning illuminated the Circle Cinema's giant entryway, displaying for us the dark and barren inside. It was easy to see why Bertucci had picked this place, as though he and the building shared a spirit: cool, retro, sort of closed up but appealing. He'd been the one to orchestrate most of our outings here. In the blue halo of light, he was impossible to ignore.

"Freaked you out, didn't I?"

Codman

I was never good at endings. Witness my proclivity for pressing *repeat* on songs, eating leftovers until they are beyond expired, and the need I had to drag the night out as long as possible, lingering in the deserted parking lot with the ragged trees, their limbs bending with each rainy gust.

It wasn't just that we were about to cap-'n'-gown it. More that I felt as though we—the three of us—were standing on a precipice, and I had no idea who—or what—was on the other side. I also had no idea how to get across. Possibly this is a shit-ass metaphor I'd have been better off editing out of existence.

Olivia whispered something I didn't catch. Her shirt was soaked through, so I was sorry to see Bertucci's old sweater appear because it covered up her epic chest and also because, like so many things Bertucci did, it made me look like a dick. I was the guy who hadn't offered her something warm to wear. "Fucking Bertucci. Leave it to you to nearly miss your own farewell party."

"It's now or never. *Allons-y?*" I asked. Olivia looked

different—not just because I hadn't laid eyes on her in a while but because she had changed. It was inevitable, I guess, and maybe if I'd been by her side more recently it wouldn't have been so obvious, but she was older somehow. Not withdrawn, but more mature. Worn.

"Lest we forget you speak French," Olivia winced. Bertucci rolled his eyes.

"*C'est vrai*, I do speak of this language."

"Okay, *frère*," Olivia nudged me in the butt with her knee. I liked that she still felt able to touch me even though I'd been the one to pull away the last time we had hugged. And when did I get to be her brother? Or maybe *frère* was just the first French word that popped into her mind. Fuck me.

The Circle appeared to have been designed by someone who was Greek or drunk or both. The original building was a cinderblock box that gave all the appeal of a jail. Over the years, considerable effort had gone into hiding the building's boxy essence. There were columns—too many to be structurally necessary—and vacant platforms where large potted plants used to be. Large windows had been added at the front, possibly so that when you stood in line to buy tickets, you didn't feel trapped. Exterior stairs had sprouted haphazardly for emergency egress, and various coats of paint inevitably flaked off in the summer heat. It was pretty much a mess.

I cupped my hands on one of the windows. A wrecking crew had started tearing the Sheetrock down inside, and a few pockmarked ceiling squares dangled down. It occurred to me that this outing might not be the best idea, but I knew we had to go through with it. I owed him at least that much.

I yanked on the door, surprised and then not. "Locked, in fact."

I could practically feel Bertucci's glare behind me, the same look he'd given our fetal pig before we'd dissected it. "Uh, yeah, because it's late, closed, and about to be condemned."

"It's not condemned," Olivia said. She pressed her hands to the glass and peered inside then jerked back like she'd seen something bad. "It's just going out of business. Like everything else in this town."

Of course Bertucci had thought ahead, or at least it seemed that way, and he led us around the side of the building where the overhang sheltered us from the deluge and the doors were held closed with a chain.

And of course, tucked behind one of the concrete angles were bolt cutters.

"Bertucci thinks of of everything," I said. "Nutbarrel."

"Bertucci, my hero," Olivia said but looked at me while she said it. I knew she'd texted him before, but it was too weird to bring that up. Who am I to say who she should and shouldn't auto-correct with?

The chains around the door were kind of pathetic. If it hadn't been pouring or night or our last adventure as a threesome, maybe it would have felt lame. But when we snipped through the metal and the lock slid to the ground, it was kind of a brave moment. And I was glad he'd been the one to suggest we do it, and glad I'd been the one to cut the proverbial chain.

"My friends." Bertucci had said this every time we'd met here. His arms were ridiculously long, and he was forever gesturing with them, sort of a demented mayor.

I fought the urge to shiver. The rain had made my hair flop down over one eye; rivulets ran down my face. I put my hand on the U-shaped door handle. My hands were girly compared to Bertucci's. "Once we go in, there's no turning back." Bertucci thought I owed him hours for a day I didn't like to think about, and now he was claiming my time. Eight hours. No matter what. A guy code? Sort of. Maybe I did owe him.

"At least there'll be Junior Mints," Olivia said. Bertucci ignored her. He let Olivia get away with any comment, every arm thwack, every change of plans. Maybe it seemed that way because I was inclined to let her get away with nothing.

Bertucci gripped the door like he was fighting against gravity or something.

"Enough drama," I said and pushed him aside—not an easy thing since he's got a half-foot on me easy and his presence towers over everything—and opened the door.

Bertucci

In AP Bio, Codman and I ended up partners for the fetal pig dissection. That wasn't his plan—being partners—but that's how it went down. I wasn't all that into investigating the innards of some creature who'd hardly had a shot at being alive, but Codman practically leaped into my lap.

"Hang back," I'd told him. "Wait."

The girls who either actually felt sickened at the thought of the dissection or just thought they had a shot at getting out of the lab clustered by Ms. Finnerman's desk. I figured if I looked like I wasn't doing anything, Finnerman might partner me with one of these delicate creatures. One thing might lead to another. Not that I'd follow through, but still.

Codman was nothing if not clueless, though. He claimed a lab table and pig in a tray in our names and grabbed the scalpel, before I even had a chance to inch closer to Livvy's friend Marta or Florida Kessler. I had a little thing for Florida. She was oddly pretty, with a small face and nice hips. She also shaved the underside of her hair. One day she'd be all nice-girl-in-a-button-down-sweater and the next she'd pull her ropey hair up, showcasing her half-shaved head. It was like she was two girls in one. . . .

But Codman's overt enthusiasm for dissection made sure I didn't wind up anywhere near Florida or her hair. Instead, Codman and I worked our way through the ten-page lab. Well, I worked, mostly in my head and a couple pages ahead of Codman, who eventually gave up after the novelty of the scalpel wore off and the tedium of the worksheet set it in. I knew I'd let him copy whenever I decided to fill in my own. People—the Gleason Scholarship committee, for example— were drawn to my work ethic for a reason.

● ● ● ●

"First things first," Livvy said. Her voice was wobbly, like she was scared or cold or both, but she tried to cover her nerves by slipping behind the first of the snack counters. "Bertucci, let me guess—Junior Mints?"

I was about to say something disarming about a welcome change of pace, but Codman corrected her first.

"Twizzlers for Bertucci, of course."

Livvy frowned. It occurred to me then that she wanted to be the one who knew my go-to candy, that maybe she and Codman competed that way. Or maybe she'd just forgotten.

"Here—allow me." I joined her behind the counter, fumbling around the fake butter vats in search of popcorn kernels while Olivia eyed me and the paraphrenalia with interest.

"You're not seriously thinking of making popcorn, are you?" Codman shook another box of sugar-crusted whatev- ers into the popcorn tub.

I shrugged. I hadn't been planning on it, but everything from Codman sounded like a dare, as though he couldn't quite believe I would be able to do much of anything.

"Not yet." Livvy pushed herself between the popcorn maker and me, the dampness of her—my—sweater tangible. "Besides, popcorn's more like our main course. We have all night to eat, let's just get hors d'oeuvres now."

"I assume the French was for my benefit," Codman said. He was frowning into a box Sno-Caps.

"The hors part was," Livvy said and grinned at me.

She had this way of smiling that I liked to think was unique to her smiling at me. That somehow her smiling at me made everything feel better, more normal.

Lightning flashed and Livvy shuddered. "Christ, I'm already freaked out," Livvy said, a little too loud. "I mean, how sad is that? The girl is scared. Ugh."

"It's not your fault you're a walking cliché," Codman said. He put a small popcorn bag on his head. I tried to swipe it off his head but he ducked.

"Let's think about this for a second," I said. "Livvy, you're only weirded out because it's night, right?"

"It's not just that it's night," she continued. "I mean, let's be real, this is trespassing. It's . . . illegal. Like what we're doing now is against the law. Permanent record kind of thing. Plus, you know . . ." She let her voice trail off. Neither of us continued for her.

I leaned on the glass counter, looking down at the boxes of candy. It was depressing that all of it was still organized. No one had thought to clear it. Maybe you can't resell candy that's been under heat lights for God knows how long, but looking at the rows of brightly colored boxes that were supposed to be treats, even at nearly five bucks a pop, I felt empty. "So we've got night, criminality, what else?"

We sat, not saying much else until Codman snapped his fingers. "Motive?"

Livvy

Did we have to go in? No. Did I *feel* like we had to? Yes. But why?

Bertucci's e-mail in my back pocket made certain I knew the night was for keeps.

Bertucci was always going on about how you have two selves, the one who wants to be a certain way and the one who just is. And how in life it's really your job to merge the two. But all I knew, standing there with Bertucci's soaking-wet sweater arms stretched nearly to the floor, was that I was terrified. And also that I had to tough it out. I'd dealt with worse, right?

"Aut vincere aut mori," Bertucci had said to me before many a horror movie in this very theater. He loved Latin, the dead language.

"Either to conquer or to die," I said, leaning on the glass counter to steady myself. Fair enough, but what was the point? Why was I doing this?

"You look ghastly," Codman said when he reached through the sliding door into the popcorn popper.

I tried not to be wounded, but there were my two selves again: the one who wished desperately to have Codman think I looked beautiful all rain-wet in an oversized sweater, and the one who wanted not to care. "Well, I do my best," I told him. "Plus, you're the one eating beyond-expired popcorn."

"This shit's so industrial it has no expiration date," Codman said and flicked a piece up in the air.

"Well, I have one," Bertucci said. He leaned on the display case with his arms crossed, eyeing us coolly.

"One what?" Codman asked, shaking a box of chocolate-covered cookie dough bites as though warding off evil spirits.

I was pretty sure I was going to throw up if we didn't just get on with this. "Are you going to do that all night?" I asked Codman as he shook another box.

"Do what?" Codman asked. He stopped right in front of me, so close I could smell his breath. So close I could have leaned in and—once and for all—felt his lips on mine.

"Nothing," I sighed. "We need to come up with a plan. Unless . . . do we have one?" I looked to see where Bertucci might want to go next. The long, black corridor under the sign that read "Theaters 1–5"? Or upstairs to the pathetic art gallery with white plastic patio furniture?

I turned back to the candy counter. Maybe I'd just stuff myself full of old Sno-Caps. I took out a movie-sized box of Twizzlers and set them on the counter for Bertucci. Bertucci was capable of eating massive quantities. I'd seen Bertucci's great buffalo chicken wing extravaganza. I'd competed with him in the late night marshmallow-in-the-mouth competition at Codman's. He sang along, mouth full of marshmallows, to that Elvis Costello record, messing up the lyrics so *murder* sounded like *mustard*, *pretending* like *preventing*. Codman wimped out of our competition, instead watching as Bertucci and I had shoved marshmallows into our mouths while the lyrics spun all around us. In a moment of either pure competition or maybe desire, Bertucci had grabbed the plastic marshmallow bag from me and then reached for my face. One by one he tucked more marshmallows into my mouth, pudging out my cheeks rodent-style, slipping one between my gums and upper lip. I blushed because it was hard work keeping the stupid marshmallows in without choking, but also because Bertucci's large hand on my face felt good. His oddly gray eyes fixed onto mine, and the song and Codman and even the silly stunt we were pulling faded into the background. Bertucci continued to feed me. But in the end, he won. Not that he ever said as much. I counted the saliva-coated marshmallows and knew I'd lost. But it didn't matter. When I really tried, I could still feel his hands on my face.

"So where to first, Nutwit?" Codman asked, his voice billowing in the empty lobby. He and Bertucci had not yet exhausted their nut names despite years of calling each other every nut word known to man. "Wherefore art thou, Nut Mitten?"

Then, before anyone else could answer, Codman said, "Retract that question. I gotta whiz." He walked away from the refreshment stand, considering the options. Men's room down the long, barren hallway alone, or women's room right here.

"I couldn't care less!" I yelled.

Codman was through the closer door in an instant.

"Bladder of a squirrel," I said. My words echoed. Out of habit, I reached for my phone. I kind of already felt like ditching. How bad was that? Not even ten minutes and I was ready for the safety and comforts of my bedroom, away from the rain and dark and the confusion of being with the boys who haunted my brain.

I pulled the paper out from my back pocket and studied it.

[The Winter of Our Discontent/Spring Awakening/
Whatever Date Cracks Your Nut]

Dear Friends,
   Greetings and Salutations!
   As you know, graduation is June 12th. We owe it
to ourselves to pull one more all-nighter. Haven't we
always talked about leaving our marks on the world?
   Here's the plan: we meet at 10:00 p.m. at the Circle
Cinema for one last hurrah. We manage to get inside
and once we're there, we tough it out until daybreak.
Relax, Livvy—it's closed but not condemned—not yet.
No panicking, no wussing-out, no leaving just because
things are tough (um, Codman, this means you). No
calling for help. Because we won't need it. We have each
other, right?
   At some point during the night you will want
to exit, but this is NOT an option. If you accept my
invitation to this event, you are agreeing to my terms.
No one says you have to show up, but if you do, you're in
till dawn.
   Hope to see you there!
   —Bertucci

"Well-written and to the point," I said, wandering near the ticket-ripper's stand. The e-mail was dated a while back but sent today, in typical Bertucci planning fashion. "Clever."

Bertucci leaned against the counter like he was considering paying for the Twizzlers or telling me a secret. Bertucci had that kind of intensity. A way of looking at you too hard or for too long, giving meaning to moments that might not be meaningful at all. A way of being with you and away from you at the same time.

"I miss you, Bertucci." The words slipped out of my mouth before I could stop them. I folded the paper and slipped it back in my pocket.

"Me too," Bertucci whispered right as the women's bathroom door squeaked open.

Codman wiped his hands on his jeans. "What'd I miss?"

5

Codman

I barely gripped the banister as I took the stairs two by two up to the Circle's gallery to check out the disastrously bad artwork. Olivia could hang out at the concession stand talking to herself all night if she wanted.

"They never sold any of it, right?" I asked. Bertucci nodded. "I mean, what if that's your life, painting shitty watercolors that hang in the Circle Cinema?"

I looked over my shoulder and saw Olivia bite her lip as she climbed the steps. Bertucci walked behind us both.

"Isn't showing pathetic art here better than never showing it at all?" she asked.

"Better to have loved and lost and all that?" I asked and felt the cold coming off of Bertucci as he went around us and skulked in between the paintings and the potted plants left withering. Spider ferns, I recognized them. The same kind Bertucci had on the windowsills in the kitchen. After his mother had died, he'd taken on the responsibility of caring for the plants, watering them, pruning them in a mechanical kind of way with miniature scissors. We'd be over at his house talking about which pizza place to order from and he'd be in there with these tiny shears, snipping away and reminding us it was his turn to choose and for the love of fuck could it please not be pizza for the obvious reason that he couldn't digest it. At the top of the stairs, I laughed at the image of such a big person snipping such little plants with tiny scissors. We'd go off to college and the plants would dry up, sitting there on the windowsill like a sign we'd all moved on.

Bertucci stopped by a watercolor of a sad clown. I pointed to it. "Hey, it's a picture of Bertucci!" I pulled my eyes down and made an exaggerated frown.

"Shut up," Oliva said and her eyes looked wounded, as if I'd overstepped a boundary. But then she added, "You know I have a thing."

I did know. Olivia hated clowns, parades, and just about anything circus-like. Regardless, I liked to give her a hard time. Possibly this said more about me than about her.

Bertucci kept his eyes on me as he walked closer to Olivia, whispering into her ear. She laughed aloud, conspiratorially. He'd e-mailed her? Why? I figured she'd have seen the yearbook, but possibly she'd put it away without looking at it, afraid of nostalgia.

So was I jealous of the e-mail? How could I be?

On the other hand, maybe. Bertucci lived on the other side of town, the wrong side, if you want to be honest, and he took many of his classes at Brookville College because our high school just wasn't challenging enough. As a result, Oliva and I hung out more just the two of us. Or else I was with Lissa Matthews until I'd put an end to that a few weeks before.

Olivia knew I'd broken up with Lissa but not exactly why, and I still hadn't told Olivia where I'd been the last couple of weeks, why I'd pushed her away. But I planned to tell her later, once the timing seemed right.

My wet shoes squeaked on the tiles, making Olivia shriek. I tripped over one of the ancient potted plants.

"Watch it," she said, "or we'll ruin the skeletal ficus."

"Band name!" the three of us overlapped and Bertucci took over.

"Live from London, Skeletal Ficus!"

I shook my head. "They sound Swedish."

Livvy nodded, clearly wanting to keep this going. "Swedish New Wave with decidedly Beach Boys undertones cleverly masked by eyeliner and Chuck Taylors."

"Impressive." It wasn't just that Livvy was built like a girl from a video game and wore ratty eighties band T-shirts pilfered from her father. Her face was neat, no makeup; her hair, a defeated shade of blonde, was always back in a complicated tangle except for the lighter bits at the front that never stayed put. Her mother hated her style—or lack thereof—but it was this absence of caring that suited her so well. Everything soft and worn. Even bedraggled and rain-damp, I couldn't look away from her.

Bertucci never took his eyes off her either. But then he bolted.

Bertucci

I was always prone to extremes. Highs and lows, my mother used to say. I'd met Codman during a particularly high period, when I couldn't seem to turn in a bad paper, when an article I'd written and sent in on a whim to the *Journal of Engineering* wound up getting accepted for publication under a pseudonym, before my mom's diagnosis, when I'd only admired Livvy from afar.

Of the two of them, Livvy was more comfortable with the lows, when I'd pretty much want to sit nursing a latte that had gone cold by the time I remembered to drink it. Or stay in bed hardly moving as the sun shifted from new in the sky to old and near the ground. She was good with quiet, with backrubs that, had I been in less of an emotional swamp, probably would have turned me on. Okay, they did. But it was like one part of my brain—or my body—responded to her hands on my shoulders, the way she'd pinch my neck in a good way, but part of me couldn't access that feeling. Who else would drag me from bed to the Box Store and, when I literally couldn't move from the trash can section, sit there all day with me, testing out the recycling bins and swing cans, distracting employees with questions about foot pedals and storage solutions? We sat there in the fluorescent light, a rainbow of empty plastic containers around us, and Livvy let me be still. Cross-legged on the industrial carpet, she didn't ask me to explain, just gave me objects to examine as though I were an archaeologist, someone visiting from another planet or time. Not once did she rush me; she was nothing if not determined.

Eventually, something would give, and Livvy would know the mood had passed, and we'd do something banal, like tacos. "Fiesta time?" she'd mouth in class, and I'd nod. Codman would be relieved, snap his fingers like a short flamenco dancer, and we'd be off.

The Circle Cinema plan tugged me out of my last pit of despair. Ideas could do that. Sometimes it was a specific thing that snapped me out of it. Other times the vapor just dissipated.

And the Circle plan, as I'd come to think of it, came from riding the above-ground train past the cinema building like I always did, following the tracks as they went from my stop, past Beaconsfield and the Circle, winding up near Brookville Community.

I'd noticed the oversized white sign saying "Closed after forty-two years. Thanks for your patronage and memories!" But the truth is that I was so shrouded in my own brain that I didn't think much about it. The train rides were built into my life. Commuting to Brookville Community for classes that, while somewhat more challenging than high school, didn't really make me work. I was on automatic at that point.

And then, just like that, it had come to me. The plan.

What was Codman always saying I always said? The point of life is to leave a mark. To show you'd been somewhere. Science is sort of the same thing: Just observing doesn't do much. In the long run, you have to figure shit out, make a hypothesis, challenge it, make note of the outcome. In class, I was the hypothesis guy, and Codman was the outcome maker. Livvy wasn't in our section, preferring Advanced Calculus, which she thought had poetry in it. It also had the majority of the varsity soccer team in it, so who knows what her motivation really was.

"I have it!" I'd said that day to no one in particular and jumped off the train before I'd reached my destination. The beginning of a plan, the first numbers in an equation of some kind.

Did I case the joint, as they say? No. But right then I did a perimeter check, eyed the movie theater doors and alarm system, which was defunct and pathetic even before the theater had shut. I toyed with writing an e-mail, programming it to send later just so no one would forget or back out. At that point, though, the movie posters were still up. In a last-ditch attempt at keeping their revenues up, the Circle management had tried to woo viewers with various schemes: a ten-pack of tickets for the cost of six, matinees in the semi-light for parents and toddlers, midnight showings of horror flicks. No one paid attention to these cries for help. Really, the cinema was past its prime, taken for granted, and just sort of crumbling into the background. And I couldn't pass up seeing one midnight showing. I dragged Livvy and Codman along.

"I can't believe you've never seen this." I could feel my mood lifting, which always made me talk faster, walk more quickly. I bought them too much candy, including an enormous pouch of Twizzlers, which I managed to eat in what would have been record time had anyone been keeping track.

"Please tell me it's not gory," Livvy said. I knew that while she needed reassurance that the movie wouldn't make her lose her shit, she despised needing the comfort. "I might have to pull a Lissa and hide in your neck."

I laughed. Codman and Lissa had only recently gotten together then, and we teased him mercilessly about Lissa's inability to watch a movie, hear a song, observe a football game without burying herself in his neck.

"That's Bertucci's whole ploy, Olivia," Codman had said. "Why else do you think he'd make us leave the house on a snowy night to see some black-and-white movie when exams are coming up?"

Livvy had shoved her hands deep into her turquoise parka. "I suspect Bertucci has no worries about studying. Do you?" I shook my head. "And I find it hard to believe I'm part of Bertucci's plan." She had removed a warm hand and poked my belly. "Since when do you have a plan?"

And just like that, I had another piece of it, everything coming together.

We settled into our seats that snowy night, looking around to see if we knew anyone else brave enough to deal with the impending storm. Codman kept looking over his shoulder at the entrance, checking to see if Lissa would surprise him. That was part of her game, how she kept him interested: appearing, disappearing, saying she'd be somewhere and then not showing up. Always being late if she showed at all. Codman protested that she was a pain in the ass, but I could tell he liked her inconsistency. Olivia was the opposite: reliable, constant, solid.

"This is a miracle of modern filmmaking," I told them. Livvy sat between us and kept sneaking peripheral looks, like Codman and I were rival tennis players and she didn't know whom to root for. "Diamatos directed this with no deal in place, no money, just a great idea and willing participants." My voice was loud even as the lights dimmed. "And no, Livvy, it's not gory, just scary. In that way of knowing something terrible is going to happen but not knowing quite what."

I could hear Livvy's breath in the darkness. She was already scared. Codman made a fist and relaxed his hand over and over again. Livvy switched seats, moving away from Codman so I was in the middle, our regular musical chairs.

It was there, in eerie glow of *The Rashomon Effect*, that everything came together. That's how math works, the poetry of formulae. I'd have to check out the art gallery; I'd have to determine a date. I'd have to gain access to the inside of the cinema and then exit without making it obvious. I'd need to rewire a bunch of shit, and I'd have to convince Codman to want in on the plan, which wouldn't be difficult, and Livvy, who would require convincing.

But I had time. It was winter, and that next stage of our lives was six months away. Codman always went to Indiana to see his relatives over break, and Livvy went somewhere exotic, returning after Christmas with a tan or carved masks or raw cinnamon I'd never use but kept anyway, letting it crumble, the fine dust coating my bedside table. So I could plot during vacation and tell them about it when we got back to school.

It would give me something to look forward to. And if they didn't know every last detail about the night beforehand, even better for them.

Livvy

Just for the record, Codman and I did kiss. Once. Upstairs, at Bertucci's house, there was a door we'd never opened.

"Hey, it's a metaphor," Codman had said, and while this could have been annoyingly pretentious, I actually fell a little in love with him when he said it.

Bertucci was downstairs attempting to make gluten-free pigs in a blanket from prepackaged dough and microwave mini hot dogs. He'd bought not one but six packages and was prepping enough for the entire neighborhood, or he would have been if he'd lived in a neighborhood without meth-addict neighbors on one side and an elderly deaf guy on the other. It wasn't a place you wandered around door-to-door asking for help or offering pigs in a blanket. It was a place you closed yourself inside, locked the door, and hoped no one found you.

"What he doesn't know," I had said, "is that I don't eat processed foods, and you're a vegetarian."

"He does know those facts," Codman corrected. "He's just choosing to ignore them."

Bertucci did that when he was in one of his moods. He'd forget or choose to take no notice of me saying I wasn't hungry or didn't want to see some stupid scary movie. Actually, he did the same thing when he was in a bad mood, only then it was more difficult for me to say no to him. So while Bertucci baked disgusting crap downstairs, the smell of which was enough to unsettle my stomach, Codman and I investigated his room. On one side was a bookshelf filled with black notebooks—at least a dozen of them. All of the notebooks were filled with equations, formulas that stretched on for pages, none of which we understood. "Damn, this guy makes me feel dumb," Codman had said as he flipped one lined page after the next. "Linear partial differential equations. What the hell?"

I nodded. "Obviously, we have a genius among us."

"Oh, but look at this," Codman said, his cat eyes narrowed. "Papa done found another journal. And it ain't full of math."

I reached for it, yanking the leather-bound book from Codman's grasp. Right away I knew we shouldn't be looking at it. While it started with some long theorem, the next page was in clear English.

> *Love, or the very thought of it, slipping downstream, her*
> *hands smooth as worn glass. A pair is the strongest suit,*
> *two together hold more than one less or one more. The*
> *triangle resists weight. The square collapses.*

"Put this back," I told Codman. "This isn't right."

Codman considered it. I could tell he wanted to read it, either because it was something to do or because he—like me—wondered what was really brewing in Bertucci's massive brain. Sure, there were problems and logic sequences, but there was lots of other stuff—love, even—and he was too private to tell us.

The leather was supple in my hands (and also cheesy—made me wonder if Bertucci had planted the journal, hoping we'd find it). The pages were thick and filled with Bertucci's all-caps scrawl. I closed the journal and stuck it quickly back on the shelf between *Death of a Salesman*—a play for which Bertucci had done the lighting—and *Le Morte D'Arthur*. I hoped Bertucci wouldn't notice if the journal was in the wrong place—I had the feeling each item in his room had an exact spot that made sense only to him.

To distract Codman from snooping around or reading more, I had to act. Words weren't enough with Codman; he responded better to action, understood exploits more than expressions. I could hear Bertucci clanking around in the kitchen. My instinct was to drag Codman down the stairs to check on the state of things, but on the way out of the room, I paused in the hallway.

On the walls were two pieces of art: a charcoal landscape Bertucci's mother had done that quite frankly was depressing, all dark and heavy, and the flipside, a gloppy, fluorescent splotchy painted mess that Bertucci had done in preschool and that his parents had framed. Between those were two photographs. One was of Bertucci back when he was short enough not to be able to reach the front doorknob, his grin lopsided and his fingers pudgy. The other was from maybe the beginning of middle school. He wasn't looking at the camera, like there was something more interesting elsewhere. I didn't know him then.

I could feel Codman standing behind me as I studied the pictures. The little kid one was framed in red plastic, and the middle one was in a fake-wood frame. When I looked closely I realized that whoever had done it hadn't taken out the insert that came with the frame. Poking out from behind an awkward Bertucci was another person, an anonymous being living alongside him in the frame.

I could smell Codman without facing him. This both bugged me and excited me because Codman's scent—not his soap or detergent—his actual person smell just got to me. Like biologically we were meant to be together. So for no reason other than to surprise him, I whipped around.

Codman darted away from me like it physically pained him to be near me. I just stood there.

Behind Codman was a door with a glass knob that I suddenly felt like opening. Codman saw me staring at the door, contemplating what could be inside. "There's a metaphor for us," he said.

And before I could doubt myself, I took the steps to close the few feet of distance between us. When we were both in front of the door, I slipped my arms around Codman's waist in a gesture that—if I had to save my heart—I could always say I meant as a joke.

But it wasn't. Codman leaned his face down to mine and the kissing just started with no pause. We kissed like we had no time, fiercely and sternly as though this was serious business. His lips found mine, and I held him so tight I might have hurt him, but we knew without saying it we couldn't do this, that we could be found out at any second.

Everything changed then—the three of us, the two of us, me—but we didn't take the time to contemplate it. It was too exciting, too real, too risky.

Bertucci shouted up the stairs before he actually arrived.

We broke apart in the nick of time, both of us breathless, Codman's lips wet, his eyes heavy.

"You weren't looking through my shit, were you?" Bertucci asked, checking us out as he stormed past us and back into his room. He slammed a book—*And Then We Came to the End*—shut on his desk. "You look guilty."

Codman shook his head. He looked at me, but I couldn't tell what his reaction was, if he wanted nothing more than to be alone with me or if he wished we hadn't kissed at all.

"No," I said. "Besides, we wouldn't get any of your symbols and equations anyway, Nutlove."

Bertucci kept studying us for signs and codes. "You want to know about the Schrödinger equation?" he asked as he leafed through a bunch of loose papers.

We didn't answer. "Basically, it predicts future behavior. Schrödinger's Cat—this experiment I'll tell you about another time." The tension between the three of us was thick, solid and sticky as dough. "It's a wave equation that predicts analytically and precisely the probability of events or outcome."

"So we're seeing the future here?" Codman asked, still short of breath. Was he saying that I was his future?

Bertucci went on. "The detailed outcome is not strictly determined, but given a large number of events, the Schrödinger equation will predict the distribution of results."

Bertucci turned to face me in the grim light of his bedroom, pictures of his past selves peeking out behind him in the hall. He didn't speak, just looked at me.

"Schrödinger's Equation," I said forcing a grin. "Early eighties band with girl lead singer and exploding drummer."

Bertucci nodded, the tension easing. "Excellent band name. And of course they paint the formula on the front of the drum and are remembered into eternity."

"German influences with a touch of Italian pop for levity," Codman said, and order between the three of us was restored.

• • • •

So we'd kissed that one time and never—not once—talked about it. We were, it turned out, really good at not talking about stuff.

I wanted to, and with the last night of everything, I knew I had to bring it up. But not in front of Bertucci.

"You realize of course, that he probably wanted us to split up," Codman said, nodding to the space where Bertucci had been.

"Maybe this whole thing was a mistake," I said. Through the double-height gallery window, the streetlights faded from green to red and back again, wobbly in the rain, while we stood there. "Obviously, there's a strategy or reason for being here that we're not figuring out."

"Schrower's equation?" Codman asked. He pushed his hands through his hair.

"Schrödinger," I corrected him. I hated that he couldn't remember that, like he was losing the language of us already. "So what should we do?" I looked around.

"Relax," Codman said. "He's not going to jump out at you."

When we'd seen *The Rashomon Effect*, Bertucci was so into it he leaned forward, arms resting on the seatback in front of him. But right when I thought he'd forgotten we were with him, he leaned back and whispered to me, warning me about what was coming next. He didn't want me to scream. "I know. I know that. I'm just thinking about his fondness for hide-and-seek and sardines and flashlight tag and maybe—"

"Maybe," Codman interrupted, coming closer to me, "you should go down that hallway—to the left. And I should take the right. The hallways meet on the other side of Theater 6, right? We can see what's here."

My heart beat way too fast.

"Come on," Codman said to me. "You only live once, right?"

Codman

I watched Olivia head off to one of the myriad snaking hallways on her side of the theater and realized she wasn't coming back to the gallery. This was either because she wasn't scared like I was or because she was but didn't want to tell me or—and this was worst of all—because she couldn't stand to be around me anymore. She probably regretted going through with the night. My parents—both psychiatrists who had met through my mom's first husband, also a shrink—would say I was transferring, and that any regret was probably my own. I put my head down and focused on the stunningly ugly paisley carpet as I walked away from bad art toward a worse fate.

The hallway, like tunnels in the dreams my father picked apart for clues, seemed to lead nowhere. I tried to remember the last time I'd been here, what movie we'd seen, what season, anything to get my mind off the sure feeling that terror was lurking behind each corner, waiting to find me if I stopped or if I kept going. I couldn't go back to where Olivia and I had been, and I couldn't go forward.

"What do you want from me?" I asked aloud to no one or maybe to Bertucci if he could hear me. "What's the plan, Nut Nozzle?"

I half-expected someone to respond, but when they didn't, and a door up and to the right creaked partway open and then shut, I felt my pulse quicken to the point where I thought I might pass out. It doesn't take much for my inner wuss to break free. I had all the courage of a maxi pad.

But I knew if I passed out, no one would find me, and I'd be left to rot in the Circle Cinema which is just about as pathetic a way to go as any, so I began to recite Freud, explaining to the walls and carpet what I believed to be true.

"Freud thought everyone has these two desires, right?" I stuck out one hand in the darkness as I padded slowly along, using my other hand to feel the wall. "There's the libido—not just sex as we think of it, but the life force, like hunger and surviving and ... sex." I paused as my fingers hit something cold. A handle. I gripped the metal and heard my breath coming in shaky gasps. "But then there's also the death drive. Um, Thanatos, who is, like, the Greek personification of death."

I opened the door and found a room in semilight. Relief flooded through me as I could see again and make sense of where I was. Not that I knew where I was, but at least I could identify that I was in a bathroom.

"Not that Freud used Thanatos exactly. See, Freud's hypothesis was sort of about libido being a form of energy, right, Nutjam?" Bertucci had spent hours combing my parent's bookshelves, reading my mother's thesis, "On Death and Sexism."

I stopped to look at myself in the mirror, aware that in horror movies, looking in the mirror never turned out well—exactly at that moment, someone or something would appear in the reflection.

But no one did. I noticed though that there was a urinal in the corner, crying out to be used, so I went over to it and closed my eyes. Closed my eyes? Yes. Always have. Call Freud! Maybe my dad sighs and closes his eyes when he takes a leak, I don't really know. Never stopped to consider why, really, until Bertucci commented on it a couple of years back when we were next to each other in the school bathroom.

"Are you about to critique my style of urinating?" I had asked him once the other guy near us left without washing his hands.

"Did I say anything?" Bertucci had said as he flushed and went to lather his hands. He washed his hands many, many times a day but I never commented on that.

"Well, don't," I'd warned him. "How a guy pisses is his own business."

"And other misheard rap lyrics," Bertucci said and left.

In the deserted bathroom, I unzipped and had let loose only a few drops when the scream came. From nowhere, the human voice wailed out and I jumped, splattering urine on my hands, my jeans, the wall. My heart and stomach lurched toward my throat, fear crackled the hairs on my arms. "What the hell!"

At that point my eyes were open and, with my fly still down, I followed the scream as it pitched and yelled, a disembodied soul crying into the echoing bathroom stall.

The wall of urinals revealed nothing, but in the stall, at the bottom of the toilet, was a small skull.

Not human. Just plastic, blue. The screams were louder up close and I needed—desperately—to find a way to silence them but as I stood there for what felt like way too long, I knew I had to pick the thing up. I zipped myself and then took a breath. Clenching my fist, I reached forward and—paused. If Bertucci was involved with the skull—and how

36

could he not be—I figured there'd be wires to cut or switches to find to shut the screams off.

But as soon as I held the skull in my hand, it stopped. Mid-scream, the bathroom went from dimly lit horror factory to mellow palace of defecation. I put the skull back down and the scream came back—louder, it seemed. I held it, the skull was quiet. I put it down, same thing.

I held it under the faucet. It still screamed, this time like a drowning man, caught in the rapids. I tried flushing it, and it popped back up, scaring me again.

"Go to hell," I told the skull and it screamed back at me from the toilet bowl.

I stood, hands on my hips, staring at the skull as it bobbed and screamed up at me.

"You win," I said aloud and picked the skull up, not tentative this time. I brought it over to the sink and gave it a quick bath, dried it best I could with my shirt, and held it with me as I went back out into the Circle's dark underbelly.

Freud said that the way our minds react to a trauma is by repeating it, even though that's a paradox because who the hell wants to repeat something frightening? But it's kind of a defense mechanism. And there I was, repeating myself, going back into the dark and heading nowhere.

Only instead of feeling worse and more alone than ever, I had the bizarre skull in my hand, and it was quiet. And I wasn't exactly alone.

"You win, Bertucci."

Bertucci

I'd never told anyone about my chess-playing past until the first snow last winter. Livvy trekked to my house only to ask me to drive her home. "I just needed a break from my parents," she'd said, and I'd gotten the keys to my parents' Camry, digging them out from the back of the bread box where my mother had taken to hiding them once my father had "gone to the basement" where he kept his stash of Kilbeggan. My mom didn't know that my dad had another set of keys locked in his rusty cash box. My dad didn't know that I knew the code to that cash box, 1757, the same year displayed on every bottle of Kilbeggan. So we were all semi-delusional about how safe everyone was from themselves.

"So, where to?" I'd asked Livvy once she was buckled in safely.

"Anywhere. Home, I guess." Her breath came out in cotton ball gasps, and she wasn't wearing enough clothing. I shed my jacket, took off the sweater I had underneath, and handed it to her. Without protesting, she accepted it and pulled it over her head while I wriggled back into my jacket.

"Heat's still broken," I said as I backed out of the driveway. It was my mother's car originally, and she hadn't been feeling well lately, and that meant not working much which translated as no extra cash to throw at her rotting vehicle. At some point it would just give up completely and sit dead in the driveway.

"It's okay," Livvy said. She turned to look out the window, her left hand was very close to the gearshift where my right hand was. "I found out about you," she said without turning.

"Oh yeah?" I forced my voice to be even, though I was nervous. What had she found out? Browser history? Evidence of some prank I'd pulled at school? Counting the pills in my medicine cabinet?

"Oh yeah. Not that I was lurking or anything, but I found stuff about how you were . . ." She moved her hand on top of mine, shifting through first gear at the red light through second and into fourth when we were on Apple Street, away from traffic. ". . . A chess prodigy. How come you never said anything?"

When I was nine years old, I was the fourth-ranked chess player in the Northeast. After school and on Saturdays, I played the old guys in Brookville Square, the ones who used to be good but had started to drink, or the one Russian homeless guy who taught me the Catalan Opening for when I played white. I was an anxious kid—always picking at my cuticles and making up reasons why I shouldn't leave the house. And our house had the charm and grace of an old marathon sock, so you knew something was off. But chess was structure and planning and theory, and the confines of it made it easy for me.

I shrugged. I pulled over because while I wanted to be the kind of guy who could drive with a beautiful girl's hand on mine in a gesture open to innumerable interpretations,

I wasn't. I was the kind of guy who pulled over and asked about it.

Livvy's turn to shrug. "I'm cold?" she sounded unsure. "I don't know. Doesn't it feel okay?"

"It does," I said. I did not add, *But what does it mean?* "But so, yeah, I used to compete."

"And then?" Livvy kept her hand on mine and I kept mine on the gear.

"And then I stopped." I moved my hand out from under hers, and when she looked the tiniest bit wounded by this I touched her hair, which sort of spilled out from her flimsy crocheted hat, the kind of hat a grandma probably made and that someone—other girls—would only wear in front of that grandma to be nice, but that Livvy actually pulled off without incident.

"But if you were, you know, this chess star, why would you just—"

"Because I woke up one morning and it was no different than any other morning and I didn't feel like going to play and I didn't feel like reviewing strategies. There's this term, *adjournment*, which is when you suspend a game with the intention of returning to it later on."

"And was your break sort of an adjournment?" Livvy bit her lip as my fingers looped around her hair.

"I thought it was, at first." Her hair felt like new grass, soft and fine and impossible not to want to touch or smell. "And then I just never went back."

Livvy shifted around, knocking my hand out of her hair, wrestling something from her back pocket. She unfolded a piece of paper to show me a grainy picture of myself, little, three maybe, with my hands folded on a chessboard, my chin resting on my hands. "How cute are you?" She paused. "I mean, you still are, of course."

"Of course," I said. There's this old cliché in chess:

planlessness is punished. And I knew right then that I was planless. In chess, you need the ability to evaluate your position and formulate a plan. I felt that I was often meticulous at planning certain things—a prank in which I filled the principal's office with so much popcorn she couldn't open the door—but with girls, I was lost. I lacked a plan for what to do with Livvy or even Ruby Benson, one of the ridiculously airbrushed twins who lived next to Codman and with whom I had hooked up on multiple occasions, never managing to formulate a plan beyond each time.

"You know Lissa Matthews?" Livvy asked. She breathed into the window and, in the steam, wrote *Lissa* in script.

I scrambled for this life preserver. "Part-time eco group leader, field hockey filly, perpetual tan?"

Livvy nodded. "You left off 'kind to animals' and 'founder of Lost & Found & Found Again.'"

I hadn't forgotten the last part. I'd left it off because I could tell Livvy wanted me to disregard Lissa Matthews, which I did in many ways, as she was a semi-undistinguishable part of the sheep-lemming herd of which Codman was a sideliner. But she'd done one good thing by starting Lost & Found & Found Again, taking all of the unclaimed items each term and donating them to the local shelters so families had hoodies in various sizes, binders, textbooks, sneakers, sometimes even T-shirts with the tags still on. I liked the idea of finding homes for these misplaced items, the stray socks and gloves making their way onto someone who might appreciate them. "What about her?" The life preserver suddenly suspiciously like an anchor.

Livvy looked at me with her lovely mouth and parenthetical raised eyebrows.

"Oh. She and Codman?" I watched as Livvy nodded. Her lips twitched like she couldn't make up her mind about laughing or sobbing. It sort of hit me then that she wouldn't cry over me in that way. I knew I mattered to her, but at the same time I felt apart from the whole Brookville High scene. "And you care a lot or a little?" I adjusted and readjusted the rearview mirror as though I'd suddenly seen something of interest.

"It's not that I want to be Lissa. I don't. We used to be friends in seventh grade and, trust me, she isn't . . . No. Wait. I am not going to be that girl." She touched the steam-coated window again.

"What girl?"

"The girl who picks apart other girls because of some emotional thing. So, never mind. Yes, Codman and Lissa are supposedly an item now, whatever that entails. But." She looked at her left hand, the one that'd started this, and I wondered if that was guilt.

"But." I started the car again and felt a rush of energy building in me. The life preserver. "But . . . that doesn't mean we can't spontaneously pick Codman up from his therapist's office, which is where he is on Friday afternoons at this time, and kidnap him and have the three of us do something."

Livvy smiled.

"Do you need to get home? I don't want to impose my potentially criminal actions on you if your parents will mind."

"My mother will not mind at all if I do," Livvy said in her best *Cat in the Hat* voice. "In fact, my parents are away all weekend so if—and I'm not saying we have to, but if—we wind up at my house for forty-eight hours, it wouldn't be the end of the world."

"Yes. Yes!" I said and slammed my hand down on the wheel, which of course made the horn blare and the car in front of me stop short so I also stopped short. The woman in the car ahead gave me the finger, but I just waved to her. "So here's the thing about planning. It's the process by which chess players take advantage of their position's advantages and try to minimize the drawbacks of the faults of that position."

Livvy tried to follow along, riding the passenger seat of both my actual car and my theoretical train of thought as I swerved away from her house and the elegant Victorians around it toward the newer but still just-as-large houses on the other side of Main over to where Codman lived a few doors down from his therapist.

I could see that she minded the way I was driving, minded that Codman's attentions might be focused elsewhere, minded that her parents were away and minded that no matter what happened, you were stuck in your own skin in your own town, in your own life. But she did not put her hand on mine again.

"It doesn't matter, Livvy," I told her. "What matters is the three of us. And escalators. And eating food in alphabetical order. That's what matters."

For a second, Livvy looked worried, her mouth pulled down at the edges. Sometimes I think I scared her. Other times I think she liked being a little scared, that it pulled her from her comfortable house and her predictable existence. Then she puffed again and exhaled onto the window. Where she'd written "Lissa" showed up again, and she clapped her hands. "Yes. Friday night! Escalators! Codman. Us!"

In order to be successful in the game, planning must always be done with the existing characteristics of your position. You can't plan with what *might* be available. Only what you have. Harry Golombek had taught me that in his *Encyclopedia of Chess*. "It is most difficult . . . when the position is evenly balanced," he wrote, "and easiest when there is only one plan to satisfy the demands of the position."

(Did I already have some of the plan in place then? Had it crystallized that fast?)

"I love that you have a plan, Bertucci," Livvy said as we parked at Codman's house. We walked up the street, discussing how amusing it would be to pretend to be patients in the waiting room and then surprise Codman when he came out of the office.

"I love that you love that I have a plan, Livvy." I was pretty sure right then that Livvy and I as a couple would never satisfy the demands of any position we were likely to find ourselves in. But Livvy and Codman—and yet Codman wasn't with her either. Neither of them knew where the keys were to the car, as it were. I walked along the sidewalk with Livvy to fetch Codman, to stitch the three of us back together again. I felt the cold creeping into my bones, the blank night spreading out around us.

Livvy

"I am just a girl walking down a dark hallway on a stormy night in a closed-up theater being stupid and probably dangerous and obviously making a colossal mistake," I said once I'd gone away from the gallery of tragically bad art and from Codman. He was probably singing to himself, old French punk songs he and Bertucci memorized. Bertucci was the one who'd had me listen to "Girls Talk," that Elvis Costello song he had on vinyl. That one line asking if it was really murder or were they just pretending. In the Circle's dead air, the line ripped through me, giving me chills.

"How do you spell *manipulative*?" I asked aloud. "B-E-R-T-U . . . I'm not kidding, Bertucci. That's what this is. In case you think this is clever or funny. Well, forget it. No more. We're not playing for a mention in the fucking school paper."

I didn't write for the school paper any longer—the last issue was published two weeks before, with Bertucci headlining—and besides, our actions would attract real legal consequences now. As it was, we were still invisible to the school.

"You think your mother would have approved?" I said aloud, but softly this time.

Bertucci's mother would have approved. She thought everything her son did was great, even the pranks that became school scandals. And he pranked her right up to the end too. I was over there every afternoon and a bunch of mornings with Bee, making sure she drank the protein shake Bertucci blended up for her—she was losing weight so fast, shrinking away into nothing. And I'd washed her a little, which Bertucci couldn't do, and his father wasn't around much except for puttering in the basement.

"That boy loves his pranks," Bee had said one afternoon while Codman and Bertucci tried to clean out the study downstairs. Bertucci told his mother that it was because he couldn't stand the mess any longer, but Codman and I knew the truth: he had to empty the room to make space for her hospital bed, the kind with electric up-and-down functions, the kind that hospice brought in as a last little comfort. I kept Bee company upstairs, feeding her leftover Passover matzo ball soup with a baby spoon. Which was worse, that Bee had kept one of Bertucci's baby spoons and now had it turned on her? Or that the soup was another symbol of freedom from our family Seder, while Bee was trapped in her body? I fed her tiny bits while Codman helped our best friend set up his mother's deathbed, something so cruel and sad I could hardly breathe when I thought about it. The only thing worse, I guess, would be having a mother do the same for her child.

"Actually, I'll tell you something, Bee," I'd said as the bed got delivered, clanking through the metal screen door as Codman swore. "I'm not convinced it's all Bertucci. It just seems like a lot of planning and execution for one person to pull off."

Bee looked up at me, her unwashed hair in oily ribbons

on the pillow, her lips dry. "I don't for a second think you doubt Bertucci. He's a master of planning. Even as a boy, that's what he did. Formulas, elaborate dinners that involved chemistry and smoke, chess matches." She fell asleep as I continued a Bertucci story, but I told her anyway, feeling that some of her son's grace and skill would filter into her dreams.

Senior Start Day was always a big deal. Seniors started a day after the rest of the school—presumably so we wouldn't be bothered by the bumbling newcomers. When we finally arrived on campus, banners wriggled in the new fall wind and potted begonias from the Parent Committee flanked the main doors. Everyone shuttled past the pillars and into the familiar hallways that already seemed small and distant, as though we were looking back on ourselves yearbook-style. Seniors had their own hallway of lockers reserved for them, and the entrance to that hallway was known to all as the Senior Doorway. The doorway itself was nothing special, just double-wide and with the school logo painted on either side. But it was something, to have a door just for our grade, the top of the student hierarchy. I'd arrived early like I always did, and stood around outside talking to Lissa in the hopes she might produce Codman—they liked each other already—all the while scanning the tops of people's heads for Bertucci. He was always my savior in crowds, anchoring me.

It was good luck to stand in the Senior Doorway, lingering as if under mistletoe, and I had a plan to make a wish as I stood directly under the center. But when the first group of us made our way toward the Senior Doorway, something looked weird. "The door's gone!" Codman said in his whisper-yell. I shook my head, sure he was wrong, but by then the football team had noticed too, and Mark Denvers, drama king in a lacrosse jacket, was pounding the newly-scrubbed walls to confirm it. "What in the hell happened? Where the fuck's our door?"

Did we have proof that Bertucci was behind the hack? No. But I knew. Or at least I thought I knew. He—or someone—had covered the doorway with sheets of plywood, then placed fliers and announcements on the plywood so it blended in with the rest of the wall. The entire entrance was covered, camouflaged.

"Who manages to hide an entire wing of the building?" I had asked him at lunch. "Did you plan for long?" Bertucci had his napkin on his lap as though we were fine-dining, though he scarfed up the daily sloppy joe.

"I do not know of what you speak," he'd said.

. . . .

Now I wished I had Bertucci to anchor me. Or that Codman hadn't ditched me for whatever was down the other corridor. What was that story we had to read, "The Lady, or the Tiger?" In one door there's a stunning woman and in the other a beast that will rip you to shreds. You have to go through one of the doors. The teacher had used it as an example of an unsolvable problem—because you just can't know what's on the other side of the door.

In the narrow tunnel, I felt fear creeping up my limbs. I also began to resent Bertucci for putting me in this situation in the first place. I narrated for no one or everyone as I inched my way in the inky air toward what I hoped would be a place where I could finally see what was happening.

"You know I know about all of the pranks, right? Even that last one?" I started to laugh. Bertucci had switched his mother's regular toothpaste with confectionary sugar and water. He wasn't really one for easy gags, but this was probably all Bee could handle. He brought the kidney-shaped plastic pink dish beneath her chin, and I held her upright as she brushed her teeth. "Ack! Phelllahghh," she spat out in to the dish, her mouth angry but her eyes laughing. "You're too much, Sweets. Too much."

. . . .

At the movie theater I kept going into the dark, afraid of something jumping out at me or pinching me from behind so I turned to press my back into the wall as I stepped. An eerie orange-red glow seeped out from around the far corner at the end of the hall. I figured it was probably the Emergency Exit sign, still illuminated. The color was the same as the dried blood on Bee's lips that I had wiped down with a washcloth and gone to rinse in the bathroom at Bertucci's.

I had opened the door without knocking since the downstairs bathroom was hardly used, and when I saw Bertucci standing at the sink, I flinched and apologized.

"Sorry, sorry! My fault. Always knock," I said and blushed.

"I forgot you were here. It's my fault. I should've closed the door." Bertucci's body was beautiful and it was difficult for me to turn away. He dressed in worn-out plaid shirts, slim-cut dark jeans, and an old mechanic jacket, and I'd never seen him without something like that covering him. He was pale but lean, and his arms suggested he'd been lifting.

"When do you work out?" I asked. I felt betrayed; I thought I'd known all there was to know about Codman and Bertucci, what they ate, their grades, the songs stuck in their heads, their workout schedules.

Bertucci was arranging medicine bottles on the cabinet shelf. He did not reach for his shirt, which hung on the towel rack to his right. He counted pills and swept some into his hand, letting them fall from his palm into the toilet in a pebble-like shower. His mother was fading; the pain meds weren't working. "At night sometimes. Mostly when I can't sleep."

I held out the bloody washcloth so he wouldn't think I had other reasons for being in the bathroom with him— except now I kind of did. Had I ever thought about Bertucci as boyfriend material? Not really. My parents were very big on proper steps to a solid life. They'd met in medical school, and though my dad had moved out only last fall, they both agreed that my future was not really up for grabs. Instead of feeling like everything was wide open to me, I walked around with the walls closing in. I had tennis and good grades and was expected to attend a fabulous college, without taking a gap year, and pursue a future that "made sense."

So there was a part of Bertucci that appealed to me because he didn't live his life that way. True, he had won awards and had more on his résumé than most adults. And UC–Berkeley awaited. But he wasn't about that. We'd sit outside the cafeteria, having carried our trays onto the main yard at his suggestion; it never would have occurred to me to eat anywhere other than the sticky-topped cafeteria tables. We'd sit there and Bertucci could come up with fifteen different ideas for that weekend or that afternoon or for the rest of my life. He was the king of ludicrous suggestions—bring cake pops to the derelicts at the bus station or take homeless kids around the world by train or create a music camp for special needs teens. All good ideas I'd never think of myself but also, I realized when I saw him in the bathroom, scenarios that involved caregiving.

In the bathroom at his house, I continued to steal glances at his shirtlessness as he went through the medicine cabinet. Could I have flirted with him? Maybe. But it felt like a language neither of us was capable of speaking.

Bertucci twisted the hot water on and I stepped forward, rinsing the blood out of the cloth I'd used to dab his mother's dry lips, watching the red slide down the chalky sink. It felt so raw, so intimate, standing there with his bare torso next to me, his mother's blood in the sink, his actual mother dying in the next room, Bertucci doing God knows what with his methodical pill-counting.

My hands began to shake. Bertucci slipped his hands under the water, half–washing his, half–dancing with mine. I looked at his reflection in the mirror and expected to find him gazing at me in the way he sometimes did, in the way I thought maybe I could gaze at him right then. As if, when I dropped out of college to go to space, he could be with me. But when I looked at his face, his mother cried out and we both stopped what we were doing to rush in to her.

We arrived breathless at her bedside, ready to do CPR or call 911.

"Gotcha!" she said with a huge smile on her face.

Codman

The skull and I walked along the corridor with a renewed sense of purpose. Bertucci was a planner, that I understood. With one exception, everything he'd ever done since I'd known him had worked out exactly right.

I thought I heard his lumbering footsteps up ahead. "I have the distinct impression that your goal is to split us up, Bertucci," I said. Not that there was an *us* between me and Olivia, per se, but it made sense that our last night together involved dividing. Now that we had, I wasn't sure if I resented him for it or if I'd end up being grateful. "Even if you aren't saying it, I know I'm supposed to figure out your puzzle."

I kept walking, slowing my pace to see if I could hear where Olivia had gone.

Bertucci was known for his puzzles. "Remember the carved stone," Bertucci had said, and it felt like a warning. Like we were all in danger of forgetting the details of senior year, of all of high school. He'd changed the carving in the stone over the main entrance, which usually read: "Brookville: A Great Place to Learn!" On Halloween, it read simply, "Boo!"

I bent down to cuff my jeans because the wetness bugged me, and when I crouched I thought about how subtle about some of Bertucci's hacks were, how over-the-top others. Like a lot of things, it sort of depended on his state of mind. "Why'd you do it? That thing last August?"

Livvy had been taking an art history class in Prague while her mother guest-lectured there, and I was touring East Coast schools and reporting back to Bertucci and Olivia, wondering if maybe college wasn't for me, if maybe the future wasn't where I was supposed to be. When I'd returned home, Olivia had picked me up from the Amtrak station in her parent's BMW and we rode with the windows down to my house, the late summer air thick as honey. Olivia was still jet-lagged and hungry at the wrong times, tired when she should be awake, and looked the same, good. Really good. But she seemed different somehow. European, maybe.

"You know, I actually had the balls to ask her if she missed me," I told Bertucci now, even though he didn't seem interested. I'd asked her in a way that I have that's half-joking, and she had only shrugged. "She told me she'd been talking and writing all the time with you." I hadn't liked the burning sensation that created in my stomach, and I turned up the volume on the French punk disc she had so obviously gotten from Bertucci. I sang along in a bad French accent and thought how nice it was, how relaxing, not to fully understand what they were singing about. "I had a plan, you know, to sort of confront her about . . . stuff. Her. Me. But then—you just stole the show, right?"

Bertucci winked at me but didn't apologize—that was never his style.

When we'd gotten to my room, it was exactly as I'd left it a week before, only entirely upside down. The desk—complete with notes about various colleges and scholarships,

Ryūnosuke Akutagawa's book of stories open right to where I had marked it—was bolted to the ceiling. The red diner chair I used as a footstool was somehow screwed into the ceiling too, next to my mail carrier bag containing my cleats, which I could smell even at a distance. Olivia buckled over laughing. I didn't know if she'd been in on it or not—or if she knew how to go about getting everything off the ceiling. I only knew that looking at her and looking at my room, I was rattled. Too rattled to tell Olivia I'd missed her, that I'd had trouble sleeping because of it.

"Why'd you do that?" I asked Bertucci now as though he could follow my train of thought.

"Because I could," I could hear him say, but I couldn't locate his voice.

Underneath a fading Exit sign at the theater, I found a door and opened it only to be met by a gust of wet wind. The fire escape. I breathed in the cold, rainy air, my face wet after only a few seconds on the platform. It was hard to believe that high school and everything about my youth was coming to an end. It was like those songs I used to sing in French—and German, too, though Bertucci and I decided that rapping in German sounded decidedly sinister, not funny like French. Because I didn't know what I was singing, the songs just sort of ended when I wasn't expecting it. That's how everything felt then, that everything I understood and knew was yanked out from under me, caps and gowns beckoning, but for what? What was I supposed to do? What mattered?

From the fire escape, I could see night seeping onto the city, the rain-wet streets, the trains slowing their service. I stood there for what could have been twenty minutes or five—I didn't know because my watch was broken—watching the lights slip into the puddles, the cars zoom through the rain. A few determined smokers huddled by the bar across Chestnut Avenue.

"That stuff'll kill you," Bertucci yelled, showing up unannounced as usual. He had a habit of voicing his opinions, like a walking PSA. "Not the most environmentally friendly choice of car, my friend," he'd say to someone in the Target parking lot. Strangers always looked surprised, some angry, some just taken aback—enough that a few put out their cigarettes.

"I don't think they can hear you," I told him. I kept thinking back to the beginning of things, back to freshman year, to papers I'd written that I thought were decent but sucked, baseball games I'd played wrong, to meeting Olivia, Bertucci. "Do you remember that day?" He said nothing. "When we first met?" It felt like I was describing a romance and it wasn't like that, but it sort of felt that way. Everything ending was like breaking up in the worst possible way.

"Of course I remember," Bertucci said, and I hoped he was telling the truth.

The first words Bertucci ever said to me were "Nice flamingo." He was walking by my house—I never asked him why—and despite the flamingo's perch between the rhododendron and the porch, Bertucci noticed. My mother hated the thing and had, on more than one occasion, put it in the green recycling bin. Only each time she did this, she'd leave the beak sticking out as though my plastic, tacky pink souvenir lawn ornament needed to breathe.

"I actually thanked you," I told Bertucci, "when you complimented my flamingo." Before I'd known what was happening, we were chucking a Frisbee across the yard, trading obscure movie lines, and ogling the bikini-clad bodies of the Benson twins, whose yard was easily visible from mine. "If I hadn't said anything back to you that day, would everything have been different? Would we still have been friends you think?"

Bertucci considered my questions.

"Who knows?" I asked, my hands wet on the fire escape. "And I'm still in semi-shock that you wound up hooking up with one of the Benson twins. You know, to be honest, I still can't tell them apart."

Bertucci wouldn't tell me much about any of those encounters except to say they were "flamingo-worthy."

The smokers finished and went into whatever bar was across Chestnut Avenue. I tried to dry my hands on my jeans while cradling the quiet plastic skull, wishing the weather were warmer, the way it had been in May. Then I thought about May and opened my mouth to tell Bertucci something, but he shook me off, staring out at the night like he was memorizing it, studying it.

"Are you cold?" I asked, which wasn't what I wanted to say, just what came out. He didn't answer. He just looked at me with this blank gaze he had sometimes, which truthfully wasn't blank, just sort of creepy. He reached for the door and I opened it for him. He slipped by me, back inside the theater, but I didn't follow him.

I thought about the night Olivia and I kissed. If he'd somehow known. What would have happened if we'd told him? If we'd talked about it then. The day after the night Olivia and I kissed in Bertucci's hallway, the flamingo disappeared. You'd think I wouldn't notice, but I take the same route in and out of my house, skipping the third porch stair, every day. Sometimes the flamingo would tilt over and look pathetic, beak-down in the bushes, and on those days I'd prop it back up. But there was no burst of pink plastic in the rhododendrons, no small black eyes fixing on me from the recycling bin.

"Where'd you put him?" I'd gone right back inside and asked my mother. She gave me a look that suggested I was being ridiculous, which of course I was, but I wouldn't stop looking. Olivia came over and used a moldy Wiffle ball bat to swat the brush, but we found nothing. At the mall that weekend, we had kung pao tofu in the food court while Bertucci was on break. I always ordered one side of fried rice and wound up wanting another.

"Get me a Fanta when you go back?" Bertucci asked and threw a balled up five dollar bill at me. At the counter, I ordered my second round of rice and started to say, "Small Fanta, please," when I noticed the employee of the month photos. October was Linda Ruelle, she of pasty skin and hair net; November showed Brian Moreland and his perfect skin and wonky teeth; and in December was my flamingo with a paper cap on its head.

"What the fuck is that?" I demanded.

The server—Linda Ruelle from the look of her—recoiled.

"That's my flamingo." Even as I said it, I was caught between laughter and annoyance. "No, really!" I waved Bertucci and Olivia over but they stayed rooted to the sticky orange table and chairs.

From then on, the flamingo showed up from time to time. As a sponsor in the school play program, for example. But the real fun began when I received a postcard—not an e-mail or text but a real, hold-in-your-hand piece of mail—from the Bahamas.

Having a great time here! Seeing old friends and some family who migrated to warmer waters. Hope you're doing well. —Bob

"Bob?" I'd asked Bertucci at the counter of Lady Foot Locker. He rang up a sale and addressed the customer even though he was talking to me.

"Don't you think it's just plain rude not to ask someone their name? I mean, sure, all this time you think you know someone—even if they aren't your species, say—but you don't!" The customer nodded and slid her receipt into her wallet, collected her shoebox, and left.

"So you're telling me my flamingo's name is Bob?" I asked, a grin playing at my mouth, especially when I realized other customers were listening.

"Yes," Bertucci said, serious in his faux referee employee uniform.

I sighed with defeat and frustration. "Fine."

. . . .

Outside on the fire escape, my phone had better reception and I answered right when I saw Olivia's number come up. I wanted to tell her where I was, that I was freaked out, relieved by the rain, that I didn't like being away from her, but instead I said, "You know I have this total fear that Bob's going to get his diploma, right? Tomorrow?"

Olivia laughed, her voice muffled maybe by the lack of decent reception inside or by fear or by the weird feeling I had in the theater that we somehow needed to be quiet, reverent. "That would be awesome." She coughed, considering something. "But—what's his last name? It's alphabetical so . . ."

"Shit," I said, and I meant it. How was I supposed to know Bob's last name? "I never asked the right things." I paused. There was more to ask her, more to say, but I felt pressed for time—which was ridiculous—and worried I'd screw up with her—which I had and wasn't ridiculous at all.

I could hear Olivia's sweater—Bertucci's, actually—rustling against her phone. I wondered if she regretted coming to meet me at the Circle, if she thought about leaving, or if she wouldn't because she was too devoted for that.

"Bob wrote to me sometimes," Olivia said. "Just so you know."

58

I heard water running—maybe she'd found the rest-room too, but I didn't ask about a skull or anything else she'd found. I didn't know if she'd had spotty reception the whole time like I did, or if she had been chatting with people or texting, and I felt left out. Like I'd missed out because I'd chosen to leave her.

It was like we were trapped in our own mazes. Olivia took a deep breath and said, "From crazy places—a resort in Thailand. Wearing snowboots in Minnesota, with his little skinny legs." Her voice sounded far away and sad. "I just thought . . . you should know. That sounds so weird but I— all this time I sort of felt like I was doing something illicit."

"Betraying my exclusive relationship with Bob?" I stared out at the wet streets. The wavering lights looked like the moon on the ocean at Olivia's beach house where we'd been a few weeks before. "Bob was cheating on me?"

I could hear her as she licked her lips and breathed hard. She was scared too.

"No, more like I was cheating on you. Or, really, like I was being included in something that I wasn't supposed to be," she said.

I felt my wet toes in my soggy shoes on the fire escape's metal slats and wished I could go hug her. She had that appeal—too strong to need you but you wanted to go to her anyway. "It's not like we had rules around Bob," I told her. "I mean . . . I don't even know how it got as big as it did."

"I'm only getting every other word you're saying. Where are you?" Olivia's voice crackled. I went to answer but before I could she added, "Well, even if we have no idea where he is now, at least Bob's seen the world."

Bertucci

It was just too easy to accept everything at face value, the songs someone put on a mix, say, or the fact that certain teachers always called on the same students, or that people used words without thinking. But I read lots of social theory, Erving Goffman, people like that who basically said that everything anyone does or says has a meaning, has a context. There's a reason why you do and say and wear what you do.

In fact, I'd told Livvy when she'd taken me to pick out my mother's casket, the choices we made said more than we even knew.

"If I pick a plain one, people interpret that, right? And if I choose the Millennium Gold, that connotes something else."

"That your mother was a Disco Queen?" Livvy asked, knowing me well enough to know that humor was entirely acceptable to me at Parchman's Funeral Home but not enough to know that the Millennium Gold was actually what I'd end up choosing because it had interlocking handles and reminded me of the Millennium Falcon.

The point was that Goffman was onto something. "You're always the performer, but you're also always the audience, watching everything unfold in front of you," I told her. By then the funeral director had come in, and my right leg was shaking and I knew I was talking too fast and sort of fondling the coffins, but I thought Livvy understood.

"I don't know how you're coping," she whispered as I signed forms and wrote my dad's name on the check I'd taken from his desk.

"I'm not," I told her, and I meant those words, but she wanted to see the me that she had created and that I guess I'd helped piece together: a guy who could call to have his mom's body collected, who could remove the wedding band from her left hand and tuck it away because he knew his mom wanted him to give it to someone one day.

Outside the funeral home, we sat in the car just like we were driving but we didn't go anywhere for a while. Livvy had to go to dinner at her parents' club and used the back seat as her changing room. It was my job to keep my eyes averted, and it was a position I found impossible to fulfill. My leg kept bouncing, my limbs moving like they had motors in them, springs and wires.

"I'm not sure Codman appreciates you," I said, looking at her by way of the rearview mirror.

"And other non sequiturs," she said, slipping her arms into a top of some kind, one of the ones she wore layered with others of its kind. She came over the gear to crumple herself into the front seat. "What does that even mean?"

I shook my head and started the engine. "What it means is that the person named Codman who we know to be Codman isn't capable of loving you. *You* being the you that you show him. Possibly he could love the you that you portray to me."

Livvy tapped me on the shoulder, so I turned and we looked at each other face to face. "Is it possible that you need meds and that you're grieving and potentially reading too much complicated sociology texts? I mean, in addition to Codman's issues and whatever I divulge to you or to him. Isn't it also possible that Codman is more than he appears to be?"

I looked in the mirror at my eyes and also the traffic behind me. "All of those things are possible, yes."

* * * *

Leave it to Codman to overlook the obvious signs in the Circle's art gallery, never once noticing that two feet from where he was standing, there hung a painting of Bob. I ordered it online because I could not figure out how to portray Bob as I wanted him to appear, daring and in trouble, perhaps with a mustache or an ironic sweater vest. Bob in a protest march, bright pink against the bland crowd? Bob as a derelict, bottle in hand, collapsed on the street corner? I tried them all and the clothing in my hamper was proof, splattered Jackson Pollock–style, and produced nothing worthy of even the Circle Cinema's ode to miserable art. It seemed that part of life was figuring out all the things you sucked at, and I learned that painting was one of my weak spots. So I sent away for a custom paint-by-numbers that I completed in Codman's basement—years from now he'll probably find the mini-Bobs I painted hidden in various corners and on shelves.

But Codman, in true Codman style, didn't notice *Bob in Jail*, my custom work. Bob's coral-tipped wings poked out from the jail bars as though reaching out to Codman or Livvy. She might have noticed but, also true to herself, said nothing probably for fear it would be interpreted too deeply.

Little did Livvy understand that Codman did not interpret anything too deeply. I always admired this about him, his ability to live superficially in a way that would be impossible for me. And yet while I admired this about Codman, I also felt it was my duty as a human being to show him what he was missing. "There's a world of meaning out there lying under the surface," I'd told him on the day I met him. He thought I was misquoting a movie line and turned to Bob—who hadn't yet been asked his name—and said, "Can you believe this guy? Can't get his lines right." Bob didn't say anything, of course, but looked smug, perched on one leg in the new lawn.

So while I had agreed with her that perhaps Codman, like objects in the rearview mirror, might be closer than he appeared to getting in touch with the world around him and the deeper meaning of life, I counted on the fact that he wasn't quite there. At least not yet. He didn't notice the painting of Bob, nor did he notice that the art gallery had been just the slightest bit tweaked so that Codman, who always took the left side of the stairs despite the natural order of things telling us to take the right up and right down, would wind up just where he had and proceed—alone, of course—down the corridor he thought he'd chosen.

Some puzzles were like that. You completed them not the way you wanted but the way the puzzlemaster had decided for you. That's just what happens in *The Rashomon Effect* and one of the reasons I think that movie is a masterpiece.

When I dragged Codman and Livvy to see it at the Circle, Codman arrived directly from Lissa Matthew's house. He looked disheveled in the way that suggested not only that he'd been messing around with Lissa but also, more importantly, that he wanted us to know that he had. I'd demanded his presence, and it hadn't taken much work to get him to the midnight showing. This did not bode well for Lissa. And Livvy I had to drag almost literally.

"You know me," she'd insisted. "I am freaked out in the previews of scary movies so why, why, why are you making me see this?" In fact, I did know her tendency to duck and curl in previews, and the truth was that I thought it was kind of cute.

I bought Twizzlers and handed Junior Mints to Codman who had bought the tickets, and Livvy handed out the gourmet sodas she'd brought in flagrant disregard for the "no outside food" policy. "I'll just tell them I'm allergic to additives," she'd said when I asked her about it.

I turned to address my friends. "The reason you need to make it through this film is that it will change your life. Your entire perspective."

"That sounds bad," said Codman. His shirt was buttoned incorrectly, and he fiddled with the top button, drawing attention to that fact. "What if I like my perspective just the way it is?"

"Then I would say you are in the dark," I told him, and the lights dimmed.

Livvy

I hung up, wishing Codman had been clearer—in every sense. How hard could it possibly be to just be fucking sure of something?

I dropped the phone in my bag, not wanting to use the last gasps of power on the flashlight function. I rummaged in my bag, identifying objects by feel: apple with a significant bruise, wallet that doesn't close properly, change from that wallet, extra socks, a small but thoroughly absorbent towel, and my keys. I pulled the keys out, linking my finger through the heart-shaped key ring so I wouldn't lose them. I was keenly aware that the keys were my one guarantee that I could get away from the Circle if I needed to. I'd promised to do this, but I didn't promise to stay indefinitely. Just till dawn. After all, Codman seemed to take leaving—or hanging up—lightly. Is that what we had in store? A future of weird texts, Thanksgiving or summer meet-ups that felt more and more obscure?

On my key ring was a tiny light that Bertucci won at the third rate amusement park. The pathetic light only worked when I pressed it at just the right spot in the middle, and then only sporadically. I tried it and felt a thrill when it cast a thin but noticeable beam onto the patterned carpet. I could see walls ahead, and the edge of the corridor, and I made my way in my still-damp clogs.

The Circle Cinema was where I had seen *Fantasia* as a kid and where my friend Marta and I had gone to late afternoon shows after tennis matches, dreaming about boyfriends and sometimes making them up, having dialogues for the benefit of onlookers as though the whole world was listening in on us. "Oh, Giles said he'll be late tonight," she'd say, or "I loved that bracelet Tom gave you last week." "Yeah," I'd reply, exaggerating my eyes. "Tom is great. He has incredible taste. That bracelet is from Oregon—he hiked there last summer." "I didn't realize Tom was a hiker," Marta would say. "Oh, there's so much about Tom you don't know," I'd reply as we waited in line for snacks, and we'd crack up.

I wished Marta were here, though I knew she couldn't have dealt with it. I wished that anyone was with me. Bertucci to hold my hand, or Codman. I slipped my phone out of my back pocket and checked for messages. It was possible the reception sucked. It was also possible that no one had called or texted me back since I'd checked minutes ago. God, was I really one of those phone-as-security-blanket people? Pleasure center, my mother had warned. Like cocaine. Every ding, every notification lighting up the dopamine in my brain. I needed to quit. To be present. Hadn't we learned that by now? Not sucked into some imaginary world—phone or otherwise—but where I stood, right then.

As I edged my way from where I'd been to whatever was ahead of me, the fact that I had no plan began to gnaw at me. I was always a planner, organized, overly prepared—more practical than Bertucci, but a planner all the same. I was the kind of person who delighted in my assignment book, checking off items as I completed the tasks. Sometimes I even added items I'd already done just to get the satisfaction of crossing them off.

In all the times we'd been together, Bertucci hadn't explained much about what he envisioned the three of us doing at the Circle. I'd asked once, "But why? What's the point of breaking in?"

And both Codman and Bertucci had given me a look that suggested I'd missed a vital part of it. "Does there have to be a point?" Codman had asked.

Bertucci shook his head. "There's obviously a point. There's a point to everything even if it's not clear right away, Nut Mime."

I wasn't sure, standing there with my tiny key light, if I had any idea what the point was.

Only that I was lonely. Hungry. Wet. Scared. As I followed the key beam, my heart began to speed up again as I recognized where I was.

When the cinema expanded, they hadn't done so all at once. Instead, they'd tacked on the smaller theaters like the modular classrooms at our school, shoved into whatever spaces they could find. I had come to the odd place where the disabled ramp came in from the back parking lot, the spot where the original cinema and the add-ons met. It was a grand space, more suited to a ball than the extra refreshment stand that stood off to the left. A chandelier that probably looked elegant in 1975 was dusty and precarious, likely to fall and injure me. I could see it: head laceration, bandages showing under my graduation cap the next day, more things Codman would have to explain in his speech.

"Fresh Snacks and More!" the sign over the stand advertised. "I'd like some 'and More,'" Codman would always say when we walked past it.

Not that there was anyone manning the place. It was unused even during the last years the Circle was in business. How sad and disappointing I found it.

"This place that is supposed to inspire glee—candy! Popcorn! Slush in cups bigger than your Uggs!" I'd said one time, and Bertucci nodded, getting it.

Codman had rolled his eyes. "It's not a tragedy, Olivia," he'd said then, or maybe another time since they melded together, an amalgam of movie nights I suspected was how I'd end up looking back when I was older. "It's just Raisinets." But I hated that the whole white Formica and glass-fronted thing was unused, ghostly, like watching something already dead but not gone.

As I approached it now, I saw that as always, the stand was fully stocked with brightly colored boxes of chocolate-covered everythings and gummy animals. I looked around but of course couldn't see anything—or anyone—who might object to me eating really old candy. I carefully stepped closer, daring myself to go behind the vacant counter. I reached my hand into the shelving, worried a mouse or rat would bite me and I'd have to get shots as a precaution against some revolting disease and then I'd show up for graduation with bandages and not be able to play tennis if I accepted the spot I'd been offered on the college team in the fall. But nothing bit me.

"Codman!" I yelled in case he was anywhere within earshot. He didn't respond, and he'd never hear me if he was in another part of the cinema. "Codman?"

Finally, I grabbed a Sno-Caps box, semi-proud that I was gutsy enough to do it. I hated breaking rules. Perhaps that was the point of the evening—to show me that I could. But when I had the box in my hand, I knew something was wrong. I shook it. No rattle promising sweet crunch. Empty. I reached for another. Nothing.

Frantically I began taking all of the boxes—Dots, Cookie Bites, Gummy Bears. "Goddamn it!" I screamed and my voice came back to me. Every single box was perfectly intact but empty. "Bertucci!"

Angry and hungry, I stormed away, trying to get the key light to come on again but unable to find the right space to press. I fumbled, tripping on the disabled ramp, banging my shin against the bottom metal bar of the railing. I winced in pain, gripped my shin, and it felt wet. The key light blinked on just long enough to show me blood. My fingers sticky with it, I reached for the towel in my bag and pressed it to the cut. Was it deep? I couldn't tell. I was sucking in air through my nose, willing the pain to go away, when I noticed a muffled sound coming from the right. Voices.

I swallowed hard, hunched over with the towel soaking in the blood as I walk-stumbled toward the noise.

The first week of senior year at Brookville High, there was a shooting at a different high school all the way across the country in some town I'd never heard of in some state I'd never visited. My mother had called from her office. "I'm between patients," she'd said. I could almost see her in the ER, blue scrubs, white coat crisp, hair tied back. "Whenever these stories come out—and they will keep happening—there's always someone who hears something odd. A noise. Loud bangs. Some such thing. If you ever hear something like that, get out. Drop your books, don't hide, don't text Codman, just get out of the building. Do you hear me?"

I had. I could hear the calm tones she used to tell people they were going to be okay, the confidence she had that with this advice, I'd escape. She went on, "And for God's sake, whatever you do, don't go toward the noise to investigate."

But I did. I went with my sliced-up leg toward the noises—a scream?—a loud clunk. When I reached a door, I opened it at the same time as a woman's voice wrapped me in a shriek. I yelped in response and dropped my towel in the doorway, clutched my bag to my chest, and darted toward another exit, tripping again on a wide stair. Then, in front of me, a film crackled on. The shriek had been part of it, but the footage began to roll.

I was in one of the tiny back theaters, Theater 12 maybe, and the black and white movie playing was instantly recognizable. *The Rashomon Effect.*

I turned to see if I was alone in the theater, and I was. The light at least made it possible to get my bearings. The green seats. The same damaged one on the aisle that had pissed off Bertucci. We'd switched rows, moving forward, too close I'd thought, neck strain—and more than that, it felt too much like we were in the movie, not watching it. "No, that's the director doing that," Bertucci had said.

. . . .

The film opened on a butcher with a bloody apron, a cleaver in his hand, and a teacher with a leather satchel trying to wait out the rainstorm under the awning of a worn-down hotel. A woman with an empty baby carriage joins them and makes small talk until the butcher begins to tell a story, and the teacher joins in. Turns out they've both seen the same dead body in the dumpster out back but haven't told anyone. It gets creepier and worse from there, with the mother then saying she saw something odd a couple of days ago and, to complicate matters, she'd been in the butcher's store to pick up ribs and the butcher had seemed agitated. The teacher then recognizes the mother, saying he taught her son, and where had the boy been the past few days?

Had I wanted to see that movie? Hell no. As I sat rewatching the opening scenes, I remembered being there in the dead of winter with Bertucci and Codman. How I'd shown up with a cape and hat Marta and I had picked up in the dollar bins at the Thrifty Closet, the vintage store by the train tracks. Marta was tall and wore old sweaters over her T-shirts and got away with it, but I always felt costumed. My mother hated used clothing, saying we could afford new and that it was an invitation to bedbugs. "She thinks it's pathetic," I'd said to Bertucci, "that I'd want to walk around in things no one else wanted. What can I say? I like the discards." I'd sat between him and Codman, the dappled light playing on my cape, on Bertucci's pale face and red lips, on Codman's washed-out jeans. Codman's shirt was buttoned incorrectly, and I kept looking at it wondering why.

I found myself drawn in again, wondering why the movie was on, how Bertucci had rigged it up, and more importantly, why I hadn't noticed the scariest thing about the movie the first time around.

In the foreground, the three characters debate the murder, the rain continues, and the camera goes from face to face. "Shifting perspective," Bertucci had said. He walked me through each shot, each scene.

Bertucci kept leaning over and whispering in my ear about the camera technique and what the director was trying to do, and then he'd lean over and whisper to Codman too. I didn't know if he was saying the same thing twice or telling him something totally different.

"Diamatos made the cast and crew live together in this closed-up hospital. Mainly to save money but also, I think, to challenge them to sort of live and breathe the story night and day," he'd said. "People always talk about his use of light and shadows, this sort of dappled thing like right there. See it on her face?" I had tried, but I couldn't see all the stuff Bertucci wanted me to, and felt like a failure somehow even though I didn't want to see it.

My hands trembled as I stared at the screen. I remembered sitting there with Bertucci and Codman, the snow falling outside so hard that it tamped down street noise you sometimes heard in the tiny theaters. I had itched to leave, to stop seeing the camera shift from one close-up to another. "See, that's on purpose," Bertucci had said, "so you don't know whose narrative is the one to follow, which one is telling the real truth."

As I looked at the screen on my own, I kept focusing on the scary thing I'd overlooked before. In the far back of the screen was a face. Not clear, but a face. As I tried to focus on it, it would disappear and then come up somewhere else. Like fog, it had no features, but somehow it was a face. Behind the butcher, in the hotel window, or near the woman's baby carriage. I could feel bile building in my stomach and panic rising in my chest.

I grabbed my bag, bolting from the seat. The seat squeaked, calling me back, but I took the wide steps fast, the pain in my shin nothing compared to my need to vacate the premises. I could hear my mother's voice in my head with each step. For God's sake, don't go toward the noise.

14

Codman

The truth is, I thought about leaving. Not bolting, but slinking out. I considered scaling the wet fire escape and dropping to the ground, probably injuring my ankle in the process, and either running home with the tiny skull in my pocket or waiting in the parking lot until dawn at which point the night would officially be over. I'd be free of the Circle, free to figure out what the hell I could possibly say at graduation. I wanted to leave.

But I couldn't. I'd promised Bertucci eight hours of my life for the eight hours of his I'd wasted. And more than that, I knew this time I couldn't leave Livvy.

When I went back inside, the heavy door clicked shut behind me, and I shivered, soaked through again with the kind of cold that took hours to get rid of. I could only imagine how shaky Olivia was, she of the permanently chilled. Even after I'd watch her play tennis, she'd only be hot for a few minutes, sweat dripping from the light hair above her ear to her chin. She'd sounded so freaked out on the phone, and I knew that I needed to find her, that splitting up had been a mistake.

The other truth I kept coming back to was how we had changed. From the beginning it was the three of us. Yeah, we had our pairings—Liv would be at tennis or off on some exotic vacation, and I'd loiter at Bertucci's work, or I'd tag along when he was with a hot Benson twin, or he'd overlap with me and Lissa Matthews at the park doing nothing except talking about what he might do next. But mainly it was the three of us.

What had our last big outing been? Probably the Night of 1,000 Escalators (real truth: the Night of 208 Escalators, but that sounded lame to Bertucci, so we ramped it up). That whole memory unfolded like a map, this part connecting to that one, one bit enlarged to show details, scale. By the time Livvy had picked me up, Bertucci had a list of every single escalator in the entire metropolitan area and had a spreadsheet so we could document the length of each ride, speed, calibrations that only his mind understood.

"Why, though?" I had asked as we worked our way through the steep ones at each red line train station and then moved on to the green, the blue, and the commuter rails that ringed the suburbs. In a semi-defunct, glass-roofed mall, with the setting sun, the escalators took on a glow, and it was possible at that moment that I thought we'd always be together. The three of us, going up and down, weaving around even when we became saggy-armed old people. The rays bounced off Livvy's hair, making it gleam silvery blonde, and Bertucci's normally furrowed brow was smooth as he laughed and crossed off another six escalators on the list.

"We have to keep going," he'd insisted when Livvy started to flag. He enlisted my help to keep her awake, pushing us forward with sugary espresso drinks and music blaring in the car. "Okay—we have no choice," Bertucci had said when it was almost two a.m., and our escapades had been going on for over twelve hours.

My thighs ached, my feet were swollen. All I wanted to do was go home, lie on my bed—or even on Bertucci's floor, which is saying a lot because his rug was all shaggy and filled with old buttons and crumbs. His desk was immaculate, though. The center drawer was filled with red, blue, and black pens Bertucci had organized like an army of ink, then pencils and protractors and erasers and sharpeners, all hyper-neat. But that was Bertucci, revolting floors and crazy-clean desk. He'd be hysterical, drawing crowds and gathering groups to do something fun on campus—decorate the gym to celebrate the debate team's second place finish at sectionals—or else he'd be manic about some essay or article he'd wanted published, disappearing for days to write and rewrite. Then without warning he'd be in his bed, tattered yellow blanket pulled halfway over his face so only his eyes would show. Olivia would bring him a plant. Or read to him. Or just sit there. But I couldn't. Frankly, it was exhausting. Even the fun crap, like riding the escalators, made me feel wired, and not always in a good way. The Night of 1,000 Escalators had sort of done me in. And what was the point? Just to keep going? *Fac fortia et patere?* Do brave deeds and endure? Maybe it was too fucking hard.

With my back against the fire escape door, I tried to picture the theater's floor plan in my head. The rabbit warren of mini movie rooms at the back, the large Theater 1 with the balcony over which the three of us had projectiled stale Jujubes. The fire escape was at the side with a view of the streets, so I was in the center, near the dead refreshment area and the large bathroom at the top of the disabled ramp. I knew those facilities well as it was in that bathroom that Lissa Matthews and I had hooked up for the first time—on a bathroom break from *Corpsepocolypse II*—and also where we'd gotten together again when she insisted on coming to see *The Rashomon Effect* even though Bertucci made it very clear that she wasn't invited.

"I don't care," Lissa'd said. "I'm your... girlfriend or whatever, and I should be allowed to see some stupid movie with you on a Saturday night."

"We're supposed to get a blizzard," I said as though snow could stop her. Lissa was wishy-washy about many things but inclusion in the bizarre love triangle that was Bertucci, Olivia, and I was not one of them. She didn't realize how impenetrable we were, I guess.

So I'd brought her as far as the disabled ramp, then into the bathroom. I'd tried half-heartedly to push her away but she'd been insistant, mumbling about her summer first-aid course, checking my pulse, her fingers on my neck, sliding her cold hand up my shirt to check my heart rate. Did I picture Livvy's face? Maybe. What had Robin Williams said? God gives men a dick and a brain but only enough blood for one to work at a time.

And then when Lissa and I were done, I told her I'd meet her afterward back at her house, climbing in the unlocked bathroom window as I'd done before. When I had exited the bathroom and gone to meet Bertucci and Olivia in the theater, I noticed my shirt was misbuttoned, but I didn't care. The bathroom was fun, the movie was bound to be too, and I needed fun. Deserved it.

Home was most definitely not fun, with my brother way out of the house; my father hardly speaking, just nodding his psychiatrist nod; and my mom taking up all the words he didn't use to pick at my grades, my college apps, the paint on the porch that needed redoing, anything but the fact that my dad was texting at inappropriate hours and was hardly home.

Bertucci was in good form that night, excited to show Olivia and me the movie he referenced all the time. He'd brought it up that first day I'd met him.

"You've never seen it?" he had asked that day in my front yard. When I shook my head, he slammed his palms on his thighs, leaving a mark in the summer heat. "That's it—we're making lime tonics and I'm walking you through it scene by scene." That was the thing about Bertucci, he was always specific. Not something to drink, but lime tonics. He knew the proportions of lime to tonic and how to swizzle cocktails, and he'd execute it all perfectly.

And he'd conjured each scene and recited all the dialogue so clearly that I'd been hooked. So much so that when I met him and Olivia in the small theater at midnight I felt like I was seeing the movie for the second time. Olivia was in a weird getup for some reason that escapes me. She was so different from Lissa, unique. But work. Sometimes Olivia was work. And maybe that was why I'd bounce back to Lissa. Lissa required very little from me. I just had to show up. When I was with Bertucci, we were witty, wittier, wittiest. Ping-ponging ideas, plotting, scheming; Olivia the perfect balance for us, able to banter; the two of them somehow made me more than I was alone, brought out all the best bits of me. Parts of myself I might never have known without them.

· · · ·

At the Circle, I heard the shriek and didn't flinch. What had Bertucci said? It's not even a human one. They recorded a gull and an elephant seal, and the sound mixer had blended it. We think it's human because we've already been manipulated into the film. I stood outside of the small theater, knowing Bertucci intended for me to go inside and watch the movie—again—but I didn't want to. Bertucci could be very convincing, but it had dawned on me recently that letting him get his way all the time might not have been good—for any of us.

So I did not go in. I felt a little proud of that. As I turned to make my way down the disabled ramp in the hopes of finding Olivia, I stepped on something soft. My first instinct? A used condom. My next? A limb. Both were gross. And wrong, I realized when I bent down and found a towel that felt damp. I opened the door to the mini theater to make sure, and not only was it indeed a towel, but it was also newly wet. With blood.

"Olivia? Livvy!" I called for her, annoyed that I only heard my own voice coming back to me and not hers.

I swore in my head, feeling nauseated and unsure whether I needed to drop the towel or keep it as some sort of evidence. *Was it really murder?* God, that song. Why had I listened to that album so much? I kept the towel, and as I tried to make my way back to the main lobby, I remembered more about when we'd been here in the winter.

Fourteen to twenty inches. That's what everyone had kept repeating that night—not just a storm, a blizzard. But the Circle stayed open. Once Lissa had gone, I'd plopped myself right between Olivia and Bertucci like I'd been there all along. Bertucci chewed Twizzler after Twizzler and kept annoying me with all the film geek shit he knew, hilarious on-set mishaps or ridiculously off-the-mark reviews or whatever.

"My own film technique is just like the director's, you know, the silent narrator?" Bertucci kept talking even as I faced the characters telling their versions of the dumpster body. "See that shot?" he asked for the twelfth time. "The best footage was filmed when the actors weren't even looking, didn't know they were being filmed. The director insisted on no costumes for any of the actors so they'd always be filmable."

It all sounded sneaky and stalkerish to me, but to Bertucci it was art. That night Livvy showed up in a thrift store

78

outfit. Why? Who knows? Maybe she was trying to be someone else. Someone's quirky aunt or Lissa or a future Livvy none of us had met yet. She thought it bought her anonymity, but Bertucci told her that disguises weren't very effective.

"They work best if they inspire pity," he said. "Like those old vaudeville hobo clowns."

Olivia swatted his arm. "Don't bring up clowns. So it'd be better if my boa weren't so jaunty?" Olivia asked.

"Exactly," I said, though I secretly thought she looked great in the aqua feathers. She had a cape and took it off to use as a blanket. I'd be lying if I said I didn't picture what could happen under that blanket in the dark. The night before had been Livvy's parents' annual Hanukkah party, and all three of us ended up sleeping over, burying our bodies under the heap of coats on Livvy's huge bed, the smell of onions and oil wafting in, the comforting sounds of adults in another room. Had I snaked my hand over to hers? Yes, but then pulled away. Maybe she'd have grabbed it. Maybe she'd wanted Bertucci's hand instead. Plus, Lissa. Lissa, who would never have shown up in a snowstorm in the aqua boa Livvy had on that made wish she'd tie me to her with it.

At *Rashomon*, Livvy fiddled with her boa, flinging it as though testing out personas—a showgirl, a Muppet. "The key with a disguise," Bertucci clarified while cracking his back and stretching, revealing a tattoo on the underside of his arm I hadn't seen before, "is to have one standout item."

"Like my boa." Olivia flung it at him.

"Yes. Although if you were horribly disfigured, it would be better."

I remembered something. "I was in California once, looking at elephant seals—you know, those giant ones with weird noses—"

"Proboscis," Bertucci interjected. I ignored him.

"And this woman showed up. Really old, kind of hobbled. And she had a huge red floppy hat with sequins. Just totally out of place, you know? And I thought how lonely she looked—not just because she was looking at seals by herself—but, like, the hat was so sad all bedazzled and shit."

Bertucci nodded. "So you get it," he said. Olivia had taken off the boa and then changed her mind. As the credits rolled she draped it around all of us like some weird, blue, feathery serpent.

We watched the whole movie right up until the conclusion.

"Stand up," Bertucci demanded.

"Hey," said the guy a row behind. "Sit down."

"We're leaving," Bertucci said to us.

Why had I let him decide? Olivia stood up, glad to go since she had hidden her eyes for half of the movie anyway, but I'd paid money for the ticket and was into the story. "What the hell, Bertucci?"

He shrugged. "The end sucks. The final scene alone has been the subject of myriad critiques. Let's get you guys a double mushroom at the Slice."

Maybe if he'd said just pizza or let's go, I'd have stayed on my own. But the specifics. Always with the details. And the vocab. Myriad. So we exited mid-show and padded through the parking lot where an easy six inches had fallen in the last couple of hours.

"I can't drive in this," I'd said.

Olivia, more manly than I in matters of the road, answered, "No worries, I've got you. I've driven in bad weather myriad times." I'd raised my eyebrows at her, and she'd smiled back.

We drove so slowly that eventually Bertucci got frustrated, exited the car, and walked right next to us, sometimes with his giant palm on the passenger side window, other times nearly blurred by the falling snow. A few times he lost his footing and careened back, but he never fell.

"Are you annoyed that we have no idea how it ends?" I asked Olivia.

She shrugged. "I guess. I don't know. I hardly watched."

I'd had a credit at the Slice, which I guessed Bertucci knew about. He also knew that I loved a bargain, so the combination of my gift card and the Slice's Twelve after Twelve for Twelve made it all the more likely that I wouldn't say no, even though I'd told Lissa I'd be sneaking into her house.

I went to the bathroom—again—after ordering and came back to find Olivia and Bertucci mid-discussion.

"I think the question really, though, is whether they could actually do it," Olivia said and grabbed a pile of white napkins from the dispenser. She was always taking more than she needed.

"Do what?" I had asked.

"You know perfectly well what I'm talking about," Olivia said over her shoulder as she left to retrieve our twelve slices—no choices, just a dozen of whatever they had left before closing—from the counter.

I didn't, but I could guess. "Kill someone?" Olivia nodded. I opened my mouth to say something, but Olivia interrupted.

"Oh, please. Codman, you couldn't do it."

I had slammed my hand on the table. "I fucking could." Why had I felt the need to make that clear? Why was I competitive over a theoretical crime? "In myriad ways."

Olivia grinned but also sighed. "Yeah, maybe, but you'd blab about it afterward. AND have to pee during it, so . . ."

"Could you?" I asked her, though we both knew the answer was obviously no.

We looked at Bertucci. The caustic fluorescent lights bore down from directly above the table, shadowing his eyes.

He took a slow, deliberate breath. "You know, I actually think I could."

"We know you could plan it," I said, and Olivia nodded, the same terror in her eyes as when the butcher in *The Rashomon Effect* had wielded his cleaver.

"No, I know you know that part," Bertucci had said. "I guess what I'm adding to that is I believe I have the ability to do it."

Bertucci

"It sounds kind of labor-intensive," Livvy said as she grunted. She was whacking the ball against the practice wall by the courts at school, her arms tense. She was so focused.

"Yeah, but it's worth it in the end," I said. I sucked a little enjoyment out of watching her effort on the court. She excelled, and I had always found that alluring.

She was out of breath and came over to me panting. "So we—and by 'we' I mean 'you'—pick a phrase."

"Right. Well, which is scarier? 'I know' or 'We see you'?" I asked, studying her eyes. She never wore makeup, and her eyes were bright against her flushed skin. She had a pimple forming on her chin and she reached for it, scratching at it and leaving a mark.

"'We see you' is too summer campy, like a peephole or something. 'I know' is ambiguous and definitely scary."

"So we break into his bathroom at home and write 'I know' on the mirror in Vaseline."

"Vaseline?"

"Because he won't see it if we do it with a light touch—

until he showers, at which point the steam will bring up the message."

"What about his vent fan? You know Codman's anal about stuff like that."

"I'll disconnect it. It'll take weeks before his parents can agree on who should be responsible for calling an electrician."

Livvy nodded, sitting next to me on the bench. Our legs touched, and I could feel the heat from her on my knee and thigh. Did I think about making a move? I wish I could say that I did, but by then I'd moved on from anything like that. "And then we do the same on his car window or something?"

I went on to explain how I'd create an e-mail account and text or e-mail all day with the same message. How I'd get a few people in my college classes to call him too. "He won't recognize their voices."

It wasn't a particularly good prank, but if Livvy noticed my efforts were slipping, she never said as much. I was already into UC–Berkeley, and everyone had seen the newspaper article about my scholarship and grant, so she knew I was able to slack off. I was keen to prank Codman mainly because it would give me an excuse to see him a bit—even if he didn't know that I was there. He'd been distant, spending time with Lissa, which I thought was a waste because he'd told me it wasn't anything real, nothing but easy and physical. Plus, it was clear to me that he had feelings for Livvy, the kind he'd regret not acting on as an adult. I didn't want him going through life wishing he'd done things differently.

I looked at Livvy in the early spring light, her hair matted with sweat, tennis racket on her lap as she strummed it like a guitar and sang. I found it difficult to believe that anyone wouldn't have feelings for her.

The clearest reason for loving Olivia wasn't how she looked, although that didn't hurt. The main reason I found her irresistible was how competent she was at almost every-thing. Yes, she got As and played tennis on a competitive level, and she could sing not just in tune but so sweetly it felt like a pickax to the heart sometimes. If my mother vomited—and she did after the chemo—Livvy just dealt with it. And if Codman suggested hiking Killer Hill one afternoon, Livvy, in no more than flip-flops, would succeed, often beating us to the top. She didn't even ask for acco-lades, which I know I admired because so much of the work I did got reviewed or published or graded. Despite the fact that certain things came easily to me—research or escalators or applied physics or test-taking—they never felt easy. My whole system required work. It was exhausting.

"She's like competence porn," Codman had said, and I'd wanted to object because mentioning porn and Livvy in the same sentence seemed disrespectful, but on the other hand, Codman was right.

"Do you resent her?"

"How can you resent greatness?" Codman, who had been next to me on Killer Hill, had said as he watched Livvy scale a rock face and wave, her cheeks the color of Braeburn apples. She was great and honest.

In light of this, I shouldn't have been surprised that Livvy had told Codman about the prank before it was fully executed, and he'd just written it off. Looking back, it shouldn't have shocked me that Livvy also excelled at such a gruesome conversation like the one the three of us had had in the pizza place.

"Obviously, you could do the disappearing weapon trick, with an icicle or something," Livvy had suggested, discussing murder as if we were going over game theory. "We get these huge ones hanging from the eaves outside my bathroom."

"God, Livvy," I said, and my tone was somewhere between condemnation and excitement.

Codman spoke up. "Is it bad that I find you sexy when you talk like that?"

"God, Codman," I said. "You find girls who talk about industrial mold appealing—of course murder has you reeled in."

Codman grinned. He padded his pizza with one of the useless waxy napkins that came out in clumps from the dispenser. "Maybe the key is to make it look accidental." He looked from Livvy's face to mine as he folded his slice in half and shoved a big mouthful in. "Open for debate—did she fall or was she pushed kind of thing."

Livvy reached for another piece of the broccoli and garlic.

"Aren't you eating, Bertucci?" Codman asked.

"It's called gluten, Nutlump," I said.

"It's called I-bought-you-a-Greek-salad, douche," he said back. He didn't say Nutmotor or Nutbutter.

"Oh, right. Sorry." I took a forkful but let it hover near my mouth. I wasn't hungry after the stunning amount of Twizzlers I'd put away, and my appetite wasn't great at that point to begin with, which I figured at least Livvy understood. She had the grace not to mention that Twizzlers contained gluten anyway.

"I'll eat it if you don't want to," she said and took the fork from my hands, letting the feta and lettuce fall into her mouth. "I think there's another part of this you'd have to consider," she said.

This was something else I liked about her; she was always evaluating, wondering if she was missing something. Most of the time she wasn't. Codman beat her to the punch.

"I'm right there with you," he said. "The thing you'd have to decide is who—if anyone—you tell."

Livvy

I unrolled my ugly athletic socks from their little ball and slid my feet into them. If you play competitive tennis, you always have extra socks—and maybe some grip tape or sunstick—on you at all times. Immediately, I felt a bit warmer and a bit better, though that feeling of ease evaporated when I heard footsteps at the end of the hall.

"I know you're there!" I yelled, not sure if I was yelling to Codman or Bertucci or even some other person who could have chosen tonight of all nights to investigate the Circle's abandoned innards. "Codman!" I said. And then, "Alex!"

It wasn't the first time the three of us had gone to some relic of a place. Bertucci had a fondness for abandoned places. Those photos online of wrecked hotels, deserted theme parks with giant clown heads on their side, gardens sprouting where they shouldn't, half-built subdivisions left to rot—Bertucci could get lost in those for hours.

On the way to my parent's house on the beach, we stopped in Lakeville only because Bertucci had read about Kiddie Land, a park that had never been finished. But what we found was a tony assisted-living development called Mahogany Way, with a sign that boasted "Learning in Your Golden Years!" That inspired us to sing the Beatles' "Golden Slumbers" in such harmony in the slim sunshine that I got teary and had to turn away.

"Where are my ghouls?" Bertucci asked when actual people had waved. "Lakeville, you disappoint."

Codman and I hoped Lakeville might be the sister town to our industrial Brookville. But it wasn't.

It was like the town that time forgot, with a diner made from an old train car with prices that suggested entire decades had passed, plus real grilled cheese and malts. There was a general store with an overgrown lake in back. There were out-of-date vehicles parked—or abandoned—by the crooked sidewalk. A discarded beach ball, colors long sun-bleached, blew from one side of the road to the other as though kicked by a ghost.

At the general store, Codman had wanted veggie jerky, which I'd insisted they wouldn't have.

"You are such a small-town snob," he'd said to me and marched up the wooden plank steps. The store was all shifted angles, falling in on itself, though it was fully stocked with beer and bologna in waxy packages and gum and candy in fruit crates by the old-time cash register. Of course Codman hadn't been able locate any item that was certified vegan, so he settled on a splotchy banana. He held it but didn't eat it as we left the store and wandered to the back.

The lake sort of appeared out of nowhere, as though it had been a field that had flooded overnight and had never gone back to being the way it was.

Bertucci had rolled up his pants and waded in. "I grow old, I grow old!" he shouted. "See? Wearing my trousers rolled."

I stared at him, not getting whatever reference he was making. Codman only shrugged.

"Enough poetry, Nutter," Codman had said. "Now *this* is the perfect place for a murder." He didn't join Bertucci in the water.

"Stop it," I'd said, because I could sort of imagine it too clearly. Two guys, a girl, an empty diner, a dead body floating in a leech-infested lake no one would see for ages.

"Do your parents know where you are?" Bertucci asked in a thick English accent, his odd gray eyes narrowed. He hunched over, trailing his fingers in the murk.

"Of course," I said, though they didn't. I'd wanted to surprise them at the house since they had accused me of not being interested in them anymore, which was partially true, and also they were too busy being angry with each other or overly polite, which was just as bad, and I couldn't stand being around either version. Another part—something they didn't want to see—was that I felt like I was too busy taking care of everything—them included—to dash off to the beach house for the weekend. My older brother had taken a job in Europe. I had exams and secret plans to do a gap year working in a hospice center, which I knew my mother would find depressing and therefore neg. And I was—at least I felt I was—taking care of Bertucci.

Codman had been retreating into Planet Lissa, spending less time with us, and Bertucci seemed like he was fading. Not miserable, exactly, but like old photos in the sun, hardly showing up at all. He moved slowly, lumbering as though he wore a knight's costume underwater, almost unable to shift his weight.

"Lakeville's just a town in the off-season," I rationalized. "I bet in the summer it's all kids with dripping ice cream cones and sunblock everywhere. Myriad good times."

"Band name," Codman mumbled, almost by instinct. None of us elaborated.

I looked at the far side of the lake, but the few cabins that were there didn't look shuttered for the season, more like shuttered for eternity with something rotting inside. I shivered and jiggled my keys.

"I think there were actually Lakeville murders back in the 1970s," Codman said. He put his hands on my shoulders, and had Bertucci not been there I felt sure I could have had the guts to turn around and kiss Codman. Again. But I didn't.

Instead I said, "There were no such things, and we are getting back in the car."

My parents weren't even at the house when we got there. In fact they never showed up, which wasn't that unusual. My mom got paged to work, or my dad had some crucial meeting. Codman made tuna and pickle sandwiches for us with cans he found in the pantry, and just pickle and cheese for Bertucci, who came up from the beach with sandy hands and began to peel away the cheese from the bread.

"What were you doing?" I asked.

"Burying a body, I hope," Codman said.

"Not quite," Bertucci said but didn't elaborate.

• • • •

I listened again for footsteps in the movie theater but heard nothing except the *ping ping ping* of rain dripping onto metal. The air conditioning vents outside, maybe. What would they put here after they tore the place down? How long would the building stand here, empty? How would we explain all the nights here, this night in particular, after there was nothing left standing to prove anything?

Footsteps again.

"You know I can hear you, right?" I shouted, and I tried to make my voice angry instead of scared. I was good at taking care of other people, but I hated the idea that I might need that too. The footsteps were heavy, the kind made with boots like the ones Bertucci wore. I always thought those boots made him look like a Beatle or at the very least English but were actually steel-toed, which I knew from the time he'd gotten over-enthused at a bowling alley and kicked through the wall. I whipped around, sure I would see him in the brown boots, his head tilted to one side, his gray eyes eerily glowing.

But he wasn't behind me.

"Codman!" I yelled and then paused to give him a chance to answer me. Without thinking, took out my phone and texted them both. *This isn't funny.* I waited for a reply.

Codman pinged me back. *Is it supposed to be?*

I shrugged even though no one could see me do it and thought about things that were supposed to be fun but weren't. When I was younger, my older brother had made me go on roller coasters with him. I'd gone because I didn't want him to be alone, even though they terrified me and I loathed the physical sensation of moving so fast. I had no intention of going on another one when Codman and Bertucci had planned the Senior Skip Day. The class had left Brookville campus in early May for National Bank Pavilion Park, a combination waterslide and amusement park where I'd planned on eating cotton candy and sitting on my butt while everyone else sprinted from one sickening ride to the next.

Other people found amusement parks enthralling, the kind of fun that required shrieking and jumping up and down with excitement. "I'm just not feeling it," I'd told Bertucci.

"Anhedonia," Bertucci said. "I am familiar with the concept. The inability to experience pleasure from activities usually found enjoyable."

I wrinkled my forehead. "It's not that bad," I'd said and laughed, which made Bertucci frown. Maybe he'd thought we'd shared that idea. "I just don't want to ride the Big

Twister or Thumper." I pointed to the enormous looping coasters on the far edge of the park.

"What do you want to do?" Codman asked.

"Something safe. Bumper cars?"

So we ran there, and I had expected to drive and bump, but Bertucci couldn't just experience the ride as it was. He'd used the bumper cars to explain Newton's three laws of motion.

"First law! Every object in motion continues to be motion and every object at rest continues to be at rest unless an outside force acts upon it."

"How about three laws of shutting up?" Codman hackled but Bertucci ignored him.

He wedged his bumper car against Codman's, pinning him in a corner. "That, my short friend, is what I have just done to you."

I swiveled my steering wheel. I'd chosen a bright pink car that was completely not my style but one my mother might have chosen for me: cheery, available, open.

"The greater the mass of an object, the harder it is to change its speed," I yelled, and Bertucci clapped his hands in agreement, encouraging commentary from onlookers.

"Livvy's got quite a brain, y'all," Bertucci shouted.

I blushed, but the truth was I liked it. I enjoyed being in a car that wasn't my color and having someone feel so strongly about me—and science, I guess—that he had to yell about it. I looked at Codman. He was kind of helpless in the corner, still stuck, and kept getting slammed by all of the other cars who found his entrapment hysterical.

Bertucci's eyes were electric as he stood up in his purple glittery car, defying the amusement park rules about keeping your seat on the seat at all times. "Newton's third law! Gather 'round, friends. . . . For every action, there is an equal and opposite reaction."

The attendant came over to yell at him, and I cringed as though it were my fault. But Bertucci talked faster, knowing our ride was nearly done. He leaped from one car to the next, finally landing on mine. I gripped his ankle so he'd stay.

"If two of these fine bumper cars are traveling at the same speed and carrying the same amount of weight and they hit," he began and squished himself next to me and took control of the wheel. "They will bounce off and move an equal distance away from each other." He leaped up and all eyes were on him—he was the best show in town—and he'd managed to create this sort of jovial atmosphere. He bounced over to Codman's car, freeing it easily, which made Codman roll his eyes.

"Anyway, as my time here is limited I will close with this: based on the second law, if there's a difference in the amount of weight carried in these two cars, the car with less weight . . . Livvy, that'd be you," he said as he smashed into my car head on. "That lighter car will travel farther away from the point of impact than the car carrying more weight."

I had wound up all the way on the other side of the ride, breathless, amazed at the whirlwind that was Bertucci. I was actually happy until we moved on to the roller coaster.

Bertucci explained the flume ride to me in physics and angles and degrees, so I went and semi-enjoyed myself. But I'd flat-out refused to go on the Big Twister. Bertucci and Codman had gone not once but three times, deep in discussion in between. I never knew what they were talking about; I didn't have time to ask, though it looked as though they were plotting something.

. . . .

On those rides I'd had to go on with my brother as a kid, I'd just talked to myself aloud to get through it, which was what

I found myself doing at the Circle as I walked in my socks, wet clogs now in my bag. I found it comforting to ramble, to hear my own voice almost as proof that I wasn't stuck in Lakeville or on some coaster ride, that I was alive.

I texted back. *If it's not fun, why do it?* Only this time no one responded. It wasn't like I expected fun, exactly.

"I know how you feel, Bertucci," I said to no one or everyone. "I get it. You hid your feelings. I did, too. We all did. Isn't that right, Codman?"

I said all of that loudly, waiting to see if anyone answered, but I didn't go into more details. The clock on the theater's wall ticked loudly, though I doubted it had the correct time. I wanted to talk about specifics, but I couldn't. About how I had cried to Marta in the middle of trying on graduation dresses. It was just too much. Bertucci. Codman. The funeral. Leaving. About waiting for a text or phone call from Codman these past weeks. None had come until the one asking if we were still going to meet tonight at the Circle.

Codman didn't answer my shouts, so I switched. I pulled the e-mail printout from my back pocket, my hands shaking. Unfolding it, I studied the words again, reading aloud.

"Hey, Bertucci!" I said instead. "I'm here now. I've stuck it out so far. Now what?"

No one answered. I could envision Codman unloading his inner demons onto Bertucci, Bertucci listening. Was it possible for them to gang up on me? Was that the downfall of triangular friendships?

I cupped my hands megaphone-style and tried once more. "Codman!"

Nothing.

I felt for my phone and texted Bertucci.

Do u know I read that book u not so cleverly left on my bedside table? In case you didn't know, we already have

Goffman's books. Or, my parents do. And sure, yeah,
everyone has their own definition of you. But you helped
them create that!

Though I hadn't told him directly, I enjoyed Bertucci's
markings, his notes in the margins. They were little peep-
holes into his brain—a place that always was kind of off-
limits. Goffman's point was that we're all kind of actors. That
we have props and costumes and everything. *"Think about*
those girls at school," he'd written, *"the ones at the center table in*
the caf, the ones using the same props as the others to try and blend."
But I got the feeling that Bertucci's goal wasn't that.

I kept texting him.

U want to appear the same to everyone, B, but u can't.
U can't control your audience, don't u know that?

Bertucci's manic bouncing from one bumper car to the
next, his pranks, it was all a ruse. A sideshow so distracting it
made it impossible to focus on the real person putting it on.

I had the feeling, standing there in the murky abandoned Circle dankness, that I might be wrong. Maybe he
could control us. Maybe I was doing exactly what he wanted
all along. But there was more, all the stuff I had never told
him. How I'd pictured kissing him, even going out with him,
how I knew we would connect and then, ultimately, shatter.
How his intensity frightened me, and I didn't think I could
handle hurting him if it came to that.

After everything that had happened, I was left with
knowing I loved them both. Entirely differently, but still.
Did they know that? Would I ever be able to tell them?

I shook my head. I knew the answer.

Codman

The murky Exit sign glow illuminated only the carpeted floor underneath it. I paused there, looking at my shaking hands. Without seeing him, I felt Bertucci in earshot. "Come on," I said. He didn't answer. "It's the last night," I reminded him. "Show yourself."

Slowly, he appeared from behind a corner, more in shadow than in front of me. He knew it was the end, maybe, and couldn't figure out how to leave.

The thing I couldn't wrap my head around was this idea that everything we did in high school, anything I had done up until now, would end. Papers, tests, long-term projects, even high school itself. And yet we were expected to show up every day. When I stood looking at the world map in Livvy's room—it took up an entire wall, and she had color-coordinated thumbtacks marking the places she'd been or wanted to go—I pictured her in all these backdrops, but somehow always without us. Bertucci would be all the way across the United States. And me—what the hell would I do? What would I ever do that was permanent?

96

"You know I know you better than anyone," I told Bertucci. A month before, I'd watched him go through his room, packing things away, doing the pre-college cleanup.

"It's not a competition," he said.

"I thought you said everything's a competition." On the floor, just out of reach of my foot, I saw an object. Bertucci didn't push it to me, so I bent down and snagged it. "Ah, the *Brookville Baton*. What a stupid name." Bertucci rolled his eyes. "I know, you explained it to me—the baton, the passing of one year to the next. Whatever."

The yearbook weighed a solid two pounds and was filled with faces I'd never see again, but I held it anyway. In the back were the senior pages I couldn't bear to look at and ads that were semi-pathetic but paid for the much of the cost.

"So, I'm guessing you joined yearbook committee not for your college apps but just to get to me," I said to Bertucci.

He nodded.

I flipped to the back to find the advertising page that got me to the Circle in the first place.

Had I forgotten? No. Not exactly. But I hadn't planned on showing up after everything that had gone down in May. But there it was, for all to see: The Plan, as we'd called it. Buried there, next to the Clock Shoppe and some sporting goods store no one went to anymore.

I felt in my pocket for a pen so I could draw something infantile on the candid shot the rest of the yearbook committee had stuck at the back, of Bertucci in the science lab. I'd seen it when I'd studied the book at my house, searching for evidence of what had happened to us this year. But now when I flipped to it, there was only a carefully cut-out window where Bertucci's face used to be.

"Why'd you do that?"

Bertucci hardly looked at me.

THANK YOU, BROOKVILLE SPONSORS!

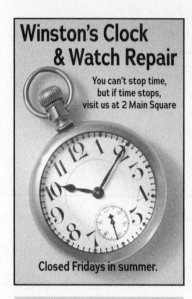

I thumbed through the black-and-white pages, the few color shots, the underclassmen in group shots, people I'd never know or never have anything in common with except attending the same school. "I didn't even get in the candids."

"Score one for me."

"I thought you said it wasn't a competition."

Bertucci crossed his arms and looked at me. "I lied."

We used to put on fake coaching voices, giving each other lame pep talks ("You're gonna go in there and order pepperoni, and when you think you got nothin' left, you're gonna find a Sprite."). I waited for him to use the voice now. "Anyway, you have nothing to worry about. You're an honorable guy. The key is to leave your mark on the world."

"Ah, your trademarked phrase. You should get that tattooed on your shoulder."

"Maybe I shall," he said, but we both knew he wouldn't. I looked back down at the book, trying to find a shot of Olivia, and when I looked back up to say I couldn't find one, Bertucci wasn't there.

· · · ·

I had the feeling, as I found my way back to the art gallery, that I was missing something crucial. Like if you had a kid and forgot him somewhere or like when my dad had come out of the Slice once and saw that his car wasn't there. He'd called the police and my mom and me and was all flailing around spewing his feelings about everything to the police when I looked away out of embarrassment and, to be honest, boredom, and noticed that there, across Chestnut Avemue, was his car. Poorly parked, because it had rolled down the steep incline? Yeah, but definitely his. Was my father happy or grateful that I pointed out his car was not in fact stolen but that he'd forgotten to set the emergency brake? No. He was pissed. Like it was my fault.

Anyway, I had the feeling that something like that was happening. The car was in front of me, but I couldn't see it.

I did, however, notice something else. "Bob!" I screamed, and my voice sounded girly so I tried it again. "Bob!" There in the frame was my flamingo. Horrifying to me was that I felt like crying when I saw the painting. Bertucci had taken the time to frame it and hang it and for some reason I found this more touching than weird.

As much as I wanted to get out of the Circle, I didn't want to leave Bob there because I knew I'd never see him again, not like this, so I unhooked the painting from the small clasp at the back and hefted it under one arm. I walked down the stairs, continuing on my search for actual people.

What if Livvy was really hurt? What if some cleaver-wielding lunatic had found her? What was wrong with me that I was trying to save Bob instead of grabbing Olivia and telling her I missed her, that I was worried? I wanted to see Olivia, show her Bob, and ask her where she'd gone in the maze of darkness.

I made my way from the gallery over to the bathroom and propped up the painting while I made use of the urinal. I still had the skull in one hand, which made for semi-awkward peeing, but better than hearing it scream. I always feel relaxed after a good piss, and I exited the bathroom sighing, only to be met with a huge bang and crashing from someone bashing on the large window in front of me.

"Bertucci, you asshole!" I screamed, sweat forming on my upper lip.

Everything was ghoulish now, the darkness, the shadows, even my painting. I regretted showing up, even though that would mean that I'd have disappointed Livvy yet again. Maybe I didn't regret it. Maybe I had the courage of a tube sock.

"Codman?"

I could hear a voice calling me from the depths of the unlit hallway in the back.

Then I heard nothing and faced the figure at the window, who continued to pound the glass on the parking lot side of the building.

I was halfway to the side door, going against my instinct and heading toward the pounding, when I felt a hand on my shoulder and let out a string of obscenities. I grabbed the wrist and spun around, angry and out of breath even though I'd been standing still.

"Codman, it's me." Livvy's voice was shaky and her hands cold. I remembered the way her hands felt at her parents' beach house, and then shook it off.

"Where the hell have you been? It feels like forever," I said, and then the pounding started again.

"Oh, well, you must've missed the part back there where you deserted me."

Bang! Smash. The pounding was incessant. "I didn't desert you. I merely suggested we split up—"

"Oh, you left me standing there, and you damn well know it." Livvy was annoyed. Her hands shook. "Shut up. Never mind." She walked deliberately toward the side door.

"Are you hurt?" I asked, and she looked at me, surprised. "No, I mean, the towel. The blood . . ." She rolled her eyes and went to the door. "You think that's a good idea?" I asked, though I followed her. "You don't know what's on the other side."

Olivia unbolted the door. "Lissa!"

"Hey," Lissa said to me as though Olivia weren't even there. "The rain's not doing me any favors. Sorry I'm late."

Livvy

Not doing her favors? Lissa's white tank top and white v-neck shirt were soaked through, making her enviable breasts visible. There she was, the blue-ribbon winner in the wet T-shirt contest, while my clothes had mainly dried. My jeans felt crunchy, all of me wrinkled, undone, Bertucci's sweater dangling over my ass.

I watched Codman—still panting in his dramatic Codman way—back up so Lissa could come in. She had a package, the writing on the label smeared and dripping green Sharpie onto her hand. I also noticed Codman's eyes take a long walk all over Lissa's top. Whatever freaked out Codman, a fine pair of breasts had soothed him for now.

Lissa looked at Codman but spoke to me. "Do you mind, Olivia, if Alex and I have a moment?"

Codman shrugged as though we were in the corridor outside of the science lab at school. Lissa waited for me to say something. Even the way she waited—with her hair cascading over one shoulder, lips twisted to the side—was flirtatious and annoying. Codman bit his upper lip then scratched the light stubble that was coming up on his chin. He wasn't going to shove her away, and I couldn't look at Lissa one more second. "Sure. Take your moment."

I backed up and then turned around, focusing on the rivulets of rain on the wide panes, the streetlight speckling the glass, anything other than the two of them behind me, probably slinking off somewhere. *Can we have a moment?* What the fuck else could I say?

No, you can't?

It was so stupid, even imaginging them together, like peeling skin from my dry thumb, knowing it would bleed, would sting, but doing it anyway. Was that what Codman was, a scab that wouldn't properly heal?

But it was hard to force myself to turn away from the images in my brain. I could easily picture Lissa's convincing argument about why they would make a good couple, how they would reunite tonight, back together just in time for graduation. I pulled out my phone and texted Bertucci. *Please come back.*

It wasn't that Lissa was a bad person—in other circumstances maybe we'd even have been friends. Even as their voices moved away from me, their intimate way of being near each other still hustling me to the periphery, I remembered a ridiculous scenario I'd dreamed up at Bertucci's after the crowds dispersed, and it was just me cleaning up. I had this vision somehow of Lissa and Bertucci together, me and Codman as a couple, the four of us magically not bothered by the cross-contamination of our emotional baggage. We could drive to the beach! Barbecue! Paddleboat as a foursome! Everything I imagined had an exclamation point in it because it was just. That. Fun.

But of course it made no sense whatsoever.

I could hear the last wisps of Lissa's giggle at the back of the lobby. The last brightness of her wet top had vanished into the blackness; I tugged Bertucci's sweater from my waist, put it on, and re-rolled the sleeves, which seemed longer now. Like being wet and surving the night so far had made even his sweater larger than life. I shifted my backpack and felt for the apple. It was bruised, but at least it was food. Then I remembered the snack bar—the first one was still stocked. Who cared about the cliché? I could feed my pain with sugar.

The snack bar was shaped like an uppercase U, with stale popcorn at the front, two sides filled with boxes, a dazzling (and now dusty) array of Slushee machines, and a glass case where nachos once roamed until trapped by fake cheese. Alone again, I felt fear creeping up the edges of my body. I also became aware of something else.

"Good thing there's no line," I said aloud. I hoisted myself over the counter and dropped down into the shadows on the service side.

When I saw Bertucci, I jumped. "Jesus, Bertucci! Why do you have to sneak up on me like that?" I hated how he scared me, showing up unannounced and out of the blue. I'd be walking along just fine and out he'd leap in front of me. It happened everywhere. "I just texted you, by the way."

"Oh, you thought you were alone?"

I pictured Codman slipping his hand around Lissa's. "Sort of."

"Well, you're not."

He leaned back against the sliding glass of the snack bar. He had on the same T-shirt that he'd worn a couple of weeks ago, a shade darker than his eyes. I couldn't see it from the angle where I was, but I knew on the back there was a tiny black dot and, at the hemline, the words *You are here*. It was like the wall-sized map I had in my room with pushpins to mark where I'd traveled. Maybe people could have those markings too, showing who'd meant something, who mattered, who'd been there.

I sank down, scooting along the linoleum so I was next to Bertucci, not cuddling exactly but as close as I could get. I put my head in my hands. Tears welled up, came spilling onto my sweatered arms, and snot worked its way from my nose to the sleeves.

My whole body shook with sobs.

I waited for Bertucci to rub my back or throw his arms around me, but he didn't. When I looked up, I hiccupped from crying so hard. I saw parking lot light filtering through the candy shelving glass, illuminating just enough so I could see something red on the floor at the other end of the candy counter. One glance at Bertucci, and he gestured with his chin for me to go see what it was.

On my hands and knees, crawling over popcorn Codman had dropped, I discovered Bertucci's iPod. He had ridiculously large and padded headphones that he hardly ever took off. "They're just so insanely comfortable," he'd said whenever I complained about their bulk.

I reached out and held the iPod in my hand, looking at Bertucci for some sort of instructions. Like I was all by myself in this puzzle of a night. Then I figured, how complicated could it really be? Obviously, I was meant to put the thing on and press play. I did, and as the music started, I stood up to brush my hands and legs free of popcorn lint. As soon as the music started up I saw the chords appear in my head.

```
Bb ————          Eb ————
   ||||||            ||||||
   \|||||            ||||||
   ||ooo|           x||o|o
   ||||||           ||||o|
   |o||||           ||o|||
   o||||o           |o||||
```

Bertucci had written them out on his hand when he'd taught me how to play it on his used acoustic. I wasn't great at reading music, but I could manage, and it seemed important to him that I learn—or maybe that he teach me.

"This song only has two chords," he had said.

As I stood there listening to those chords, I thought about how the strings had pressed into my fingers in his room, leaving marks.

"Remember when you showed me how to play it?" I said to Bertucci. "You told us that quote from Harlan Howard?" I laughed, remembering. "And Codman, in his eloquence, said, 'Who the fuck is Harlan Howard?'" I knew he was a country songwriter, but that's about it. "The thing is, it kind of hurts to play the guitar when you first start," I said, and Bertucci nodded, showing me the calluses on his fingers. "I couldn't really get my fingers to cooperate." I thought back to that day. "It was a sort of sad afternoon, wasn't it?" Bertucci shrugged. Maybe he didn't look at it that way. "It was like . . . the three of us at your house, but wanting to be elsewhere."

Bertucci nodded. "Harlan Howard said, 'All you need to write a song is three chords and the truth.'"

"You know what, Bertucci, this song only has two chords, so what does that even mean?" I asked. It was one of those questions that was meant to imply more, but I felt too shy to actually ask. I reached for Bertucci, but he pulled away, and I flinched, stung. The last time I'd heard this song was on Bertucci's ugly back porch, right before Memorial Day weekend. He had rearranged my hands and made the song come to life.

With the music and the popcorn littered around us, I looked at Bertucci and instantly remembered seeing him for the first time. "Do you remember that?" I asked, like he could read my mind.

"Tell me," Bertucci said. He folded his long arms over his knees and tilted his head to the side in full-on listening mode.

"Okay," I started, shifting on the dirty carpet. "You may or may not know that my freshman orientation night involved the embarrassing addition of parents. I sat next to my mother—she smelled like that nasty hospital sanitizer. And bananas. Or maybe the sanitizer was banana scented." I paused and looked at Bertucci, trying to memorize the way he looked at me.

"Anyway, there I was, my eyes darting from face to face. I did that thing where you pretend to stretch just so you could turn around and look at everyone filtering into the room. Mr. Griffin gave that speech. Ugh, and the clubs gave their plugs for why we would love Vive La France! or Chess Central . . ." I could swear I saw Bertucci flinch as I mentioned chess, but I went on. "So my mom's like, 'You'll make a ton of friends!' And I'm rolling my eyes. And then we're on the way out of the auditorium, and she points to a kid in purple cargo pants and a black T-shirt and goes on and on about the purple pants."

"So that was me?" Bertucci asked.

"Yeah," I said, "but I didn't know it was you yet. So my mom says, 'How bad could he be? Purple pants. Now that's a friendly sight.' And I'm blushing. . . ."

"And then what?" Bertucci unfolded his legs so they just about reached mine. I tried not to picture what Lissa and Codman were doing wherever they were.

"So . . . it's like a week later, still freshman year, and I haven't thought about the purple pants at all. But then I get out of mandatory Freshman Focus—it was How to Be a Good Peer, by the way, fat lot of good that did." I took a deep breath, the cinema's quiet enveloping us. "It was fall but one of those days that made it feel like summer? Anyway, I remember scanning the crowds for Marta—you know I've known her since fifth grade, right? But I didn't see her."

As I sat there, talking to Bertucci, so many details came back to me, like remembering a dream, piecing the memory back together. Had I begun to do that? Erase the stuff that had actually happened so I didn't have to deal with the fact that it was gone?

When I didn't see Marta, I'd gone to find shade under a pine tree so I could study my schedule. I remember I had French next, and though they were pressuring me, I had no intentions of joining Vive la France!, mainly because I couldn't deal with their exclamation point. "No, thanks!" I wrote when the clipboard had been passed around. "Non, merci!" Codman had added. What if I had taken Spanish instead? What if? What if? What if? I thought but didn't say aloud.

"So," I said to Bertucci, who could wait just about forever for someone to get a point across, "without knowing why, I looked up from my schedule. And across the quad was a splotch of color. Your purple pants." I looked at him and he looked sad, maybe remembering that day, everything that had happened since. "You made me smile that day, Bertucci. I couldn't help it. Purple pants? I mean, who wears purple pants except someone with extreme confidence or no public shame?"

"Me, I guess," he said. "And as you well know, I suffer form both of those afflictions."

"You know, I'm not even sure I realized I'd been staring. But then, the boy—you, I mean—noticed me. You didn't wave exactly. More like you lifted your hand like there was a fly or something. Absentminded . . . and yet specifically directed at me." I felt my eyes fill up. I'd never have that first time wave again. I bit my top lip. "It was a gentle wave. Friendly." I stared at Bertucci, wishing we had more time together. "And just like that, I kind of knew we'd be friends."

Then the next song began, and before I really I knew what was happening now, we were dancing.

Bertucci was staunchly anti–school dances, and I wasn't super-coordinated, but I liked the idea of it. There, in the stained lobby light, with stale popcorn under my feet, I swayed slowly, thinking of the shitty midwinter formal junior year when he'd draped my arms on his shoulders, and we'd swayed Frankenstein-style to some song he'd put on by hijacking the DJ booth. What if I'd kissed him then? Now, my body moved to the iPod music, the lyrics washing over us.

"The Last Day of Our Acquaintance." He'd made a good-bye mix a few months before. Would we ever be able to listen to it all the way through?

Was I crying? God, how embarrassing. Yes, but not hard. Just drops falling like musical notes from my eyes to my cheeks, onto my own arms and then the floor. It, everything—this night signifying the end of it all, the unresolved crap between the three of us, the good-byes that weren't *good*, just *bye*. Too much ending. I would never have both Codman and Bertucci.

Or I might never be with either of them.

This moment, like all the other moments, would end.

I looked at Bertucci but couldn't get him to look right back at me. He had a habit of doing that, looking away from me when I tried to get him to focus. "Was this what you wanted?" I asked, but as I said it, even I didn't know if I meant did he want me—us—or did he want all three of us to just recognize that we were over.

That this night was really only about saying good-bye.

The song continued, and my feet crunched on popcorn. My elbow banged the snack counter and I ignored the pain, my arm rustling against the Twizzlers that were unopened. All manner of crap crunched beneath my shoes, and I had visions of having to chuck them out in the morning. I vowed to get rid of my ugly, candy-ruined shoes if I actually made it out of the Circle.

The lyrics kept coming, and I danced seriously, like I was being graded or like I was part of the music itself, somehow wound into the chords. There was nothing else to do but to let go of Bertucci, so I did and I spun around and around.

My eyes closed, and I was dizzy and transported. I swung my arms as the guitar picked up tempo, playing harshly. I moved my legs, my arms, spinning, singing. It was like being on one of the rides I loathed.

When the track ended I was stunned and out of breath. I opened my eyes, and I was alone.

Bertucci

It was Codman who put together the handout for my mother's funeral, picking quotes he'd heard her say over the years, choosing songs she used to hum, a hymn I hadn't even realized she knew but that Codman and Livvy understood to be her favorite. Grass and lambs, find shelter from the rain, blah blah blah. I couldn't even think about Photoshop or printing presses or being organized enough to do more than show up.

Livvy and Codman pretty much functioned for me at that point. I had a big commitment to staring into space for hours at a time, becoming well-acquainted with my pillow, forgetting my shower, and disregarding food.

Were you supposed to keep the memorial pamphlet as though, like the yearbook, it was something on which to reflect over vanilla-bean blended drinks this summer?

Lissa was on the yearbook committee and as a result, among the senior candids, there was a huge shot of her and Codman under the senior doorway. Honestly, I had no recollection of taking that picture, though when I'd roped her into the night at the Circle, she'd told me I deserved photo credit.

I counted on Lissa coming to the Circle, but I did not count on the fact that, for once, Codman would keep his mouth closed and not quickly or at least quietly explain to Livvy that he knew nothing about it. Livvy assumed Codman had invited Lissa along on our adventure, and I couldn't very well tell her otherwise. Plus, even though I hated to see Livvy's tears, she looked beautiful when she cried, all glassy-eyed and dramatic, so different from her usual poised self.

When I got to the top of the disabled ramp, Codman was there, pacing, his shirt untucked. "What the hell, Bertucci?" he was saying.

"I'm not going to wait all day, Alex!" Lissa's yell was muffled from the bathroom.

What did Lissa expect? To show up here with a foil-wrapped tray of coconut brownies and find her place in the shape of us? Had I in some way wanted that? Maybe.

"What is she doing here?" Codman demanded. His hands swept through his hair.

I shrugged and leaned into the door. Maybe I wanted Lissa to prove she could be her own person, connecting in a way that didn't involve her mouth, and maybe I hoped Codman would demontrate what I knew—that he wasn't a disrespectful schmuck but a person who would do great things in this world.

"I'm screwed. I . . . what's the point . . . am I just supposed to tell her to leave?" Codman looked down and then at me, pleading. "She's actually waiting in there." He seethed. "On the low toilet, the one with the rails? I mean, come on."

"You can't be with her," I told Codman, but he was too busy wringing his hands to hear. Before she got sick, my mom had given me a book for Valentine's Day. This was so sad on so many counts that I found it hard to think about; to get a gift from your mom on a day meant for chocolates, cards, and romance wasn't tragic, but it was certainly lame.

But I felt bad for thinking so because my mom only meant it to show she was thinking of me. Plus, the book was expensive, hardcover, and she didn't have the cash for vegetables half the time, let alone new books.

But the real problem was that she'd already given me the book back in seventh grade. I'd been in a puzzle phase, trickery of the eye, puns, hidden pictures. This book—that I now had two of—was *What the Eye Can't See*, and it had overlapping images and double pictures, hexagons on their sides, all sorts of things. You were meant to have your eyes relax enough so that the focus loosened. This revealed another picture, something silly like a dolphin with a hat on or a turtle with roller skates. I'd put the book on my shelf next to its older twin and then packed it away, but I couldn't help but feel that Codman suffered from the hidden picture dilemma. He was so busy looking at the overlapping breasts that he was unable to see the real picture beneath.

It was obvious to me how much he cared for Livvy—in a way I would never be able to—but as the spring had turned into near summer, with graduation looming, our caps and gowns on order, it dawned on me that it was quite possible that Codman didn't know this. Either he wasn't aware of his own feelings, or he was and this scared the shit out of him and so he chose to be around Lissa and not around Livvy, or us. As though he was—without knowing it—planning his own future regret.

"Help me, Bertucci," Codman said under his breath.

"Should I block the door or push you in?" I asked.

Codman wiped his hands over his face, feeling his stubble, buying time by saying through his cupped hands on the door, "Give me a minute, Lissa." Codman stepped away from the door, and I took this as my cue to go into the bathroom, but when I tried the door it wouldn't budge. I raised my eyebrows at Codman.

It was possible that this was payback. Codman has burst in on me in the Bensons' bathroom—caught me in there with one of the twins, and I knew he couldn't even say her name because he couldn't tell them apart. What he didn't know is that being in no way, shape, or form able to handle an encounter with a Benson or anyone else, I'd turned Lindsay Benson down, which was embarrassing for her. And she'd caught me looking through the prescription bottles in the medicine cabinet, which was embarrassing for me, and Codman was embarrassed that he'd walked in and caught us doing whatever it is he thought we were doing. It was a three-way mortification.

As a result, he probably wanted to prove to me that he was perfectly capable of making full use of the handrails and the large mirror.

Just as I was set to pound on the door, it opened bit by bit until Lissa, the strap of her tank top off her shoulder, looking alluring enough that even I had to acknowledge it, stepped out. "I'm guessing you're not coming in," she said to Codman, ignoring me.

Codman and I both shook our heads. She looked at me like I meant nothing. "Why am I even here, anyway?" she asked. I looked at the package in her hands. She knew why.

"I didn't ask you to you come," Codman said.

"I know that," Lissa spoke tersely to him. "I figured it out—it's not rocket science. I mean, we placed an ad." She looked everywhere but at me. "Brookville Outdoor Rec and Sport? Hello? That's my family." She shook her head.

"So you just read the note?"

"It wasn't a secret," Lissa said. "I mean, it's sitting in there for the whole school to see."

"No one reads those ads," Codman said.

"Except you, apparently," Lissa said.

"And you, in fact," Codman said, his back to me. "Can't

you picture Bertucci swapping the layout, moving ads around?"

"Anyway, I brought you this," Lissa said. She held out the rain-wrinkled package, looking past me. Probably pissed I hadn't invited her outright.

In her peelable layered tank tops, she really was just the messenger. Someone to help get my friends to deal with their shit. Maybe I wanted closure. Not only was it satisfying in a mathematical parenthetical kind of way, it was also what was right. Codman had a way of shirking duties or slinking away, Livvy had a way of accepting Codman's shirkage, and Lissa had fallen prey to the Greek tragedy of hookup dilemmas—obvious to everyone where her storm of self-loathing was headed.

"Just figure your shit out already," I said to no one, to everyone.

"Guess I was just here to add a little action," Lissa said as she brushed past me and down the ramp. "So we're really broken up. That's it, isn't it?" she asked. She pulled a piece of paper from her pocket, my block writing visible.

I shrugged. It was inevitable, wasn't it? Codman didn't confirm or deny, but we all knew she spoke the truth. She gestured with the note but didn't give it away. "Robert Frost," Lissa read. "He's the two-roads guy, right? Like in English class? There's always a choice?" Her voice faltered. It was possible she had more depth than we gave her credit for, that she'd been more affected by the events of this spring than we knew. She shook her head. She'd go off to college in the fall, become a logo designer or inherit her parents' sporting store and just recede in the rearview mirrors of so many lives. "Anyway. It's just a quote. 'The best way out is always through.'"

Codman shifted back and forth, chewing the words. "Lissa . . ."

She bounded down the ramp so fast I thought she might fall.

The best way out is always through. Would we ever be?

There were dumpsters out back, and I imagined Lissa kicking one or chucking anything she had of Codman's in there. His body, if she could get her hands on it. "She really wanted to stay," Codman said softly as he held the package in one hand. He took a few steps to go after her but stopped before I even had to reach out to stop him.

Codman

Bertucci had a nasty habit of saying things I didn't want to hear—that the reason I'd tanked the Physics AP wasn't because it had a bias against Jews, as I so aptly argued to my therapist, but rather because I had not studied and despite wanting to be the kind of student that Bertucci was—that is, the kind who barely seemed to crack a book and yet excelled—I wasn't. He didn't do this as a mark of cruelty, only as a way of setting things right.

"Miss me?" he'd asked Olivia on the Night of 1,000 Escalators.

"Of course," she'd said, linking a finger into one of his belt loops as a way to steady herself on the steepest ones we'd found, from the top of the Metropolitan Building down past the lobby and into the subway.

"*Mais bien sûr*, Le Nut Sac," I translated into French, although no one had asked me to. If I'd had Bertucci's knack for stating what no one wanted to hear, I might have added that his absence had made my life a little easier. "*La vie est plus facile sans toi.*"

Less fun? That too. But also not as stressful. His manic-to-mellow moods were hard to keep up with and, if I actually admitted it—which I did but only in therapy—I wasn't thrilled about the time he'd been alone with Livvy.

This also made me feel like an asshole.

Olivia had totally stepped up to bat for Bertucci from the minute his mom got diagnosed, and while I'd pitched in where I could, I certainly wasn't there every day. So what did I resent? The fact that Livvy was a decent enough person to miss her own senior prom to pick out caskets with our best friend? The last English paper I'd turned in was on Ophelia as a victim of circumstance, and I believe the phrase *phoning it in* best describes my effort. At least that's what Mrs. Connolly said in her comments. She'd written, "What are you trying to say here?" in big red all-caps.

"I don't know," I wrote beneath, even though I wasn't handing it back in or anything.

Watching Olivia commit so fully to helping Bertucci only highlighted how good she was at so many things. And while I was glad that all of Bertucci's work had paid off and he'd gotten his genius grant and an article in the paper to prove it, where did that leave me?

"Oh, don't be such a turd," Olivia had said as she checked off another escalator on Bertucci's spreadsheet.

Bertucci could have easily brought up how hard he had it, with the particular circumstances of his home life, the rabbit holes that made up the cruel forest of his brilliant mind, or how stable my life seemed in comparison, but he didn't. "Alex Codman," Bertucci said, "you, sir, are bound for something big."

"That's not how it works, though, right?" I held on to the moving black banister and picked at a strand of coconut that was wedged between my back molars. We'd stopped at Sweet Nothings after nineteen escalators.

"Like what? Great, you mean?" Olivia had half-shouted from the escalator next to mine. They weren't particularly synchronized, so the three of us weren't riding up at the same speeds. Olivia was just behind me, but Bertucci was way ahead, as if his step moved faster.

"Exactly," I said. "Maybe some people walk around thinking they're destined for greatness or at least more than mediocrity, but . . ." I'd watched the stairs slip back into the machine; the black rubbed handrail slipping down to repeat what it had just done. "I think I just might have the opportunity to neither excel nor fail. Just kinda float."

There was a commotion and Olivia quickly hauled herself up one side of her escalator and swiveled so she was on my left, then landed two steps above me. "I don't for a second think that's true." She paused as we neared the top. Bertucci was already there, waiting for us on the platform before leaping onto the next triple set that lead to another floor of retail. "You know what I think?"

I could smell the licorice on her breath, see a gap of skin between her English Beat T-shirt and the top of her jeans. "What, Livvy?"

She opened her mouth to correct me, I thought, give me a stern *Olivia*, but she put her hands on my shoulders. "At some point, you're going to see your name in lights—metaphorical or otherwise—and you'll know what everyone else does." She licked her lips and prepared to step off the stairs. "Your life is going to be amazing—and anyone who's a part of it will feel that."

We stepped onto solid ground just for a minute before the next moving staircase beckoned. I didn't know if Bertucci heard Olivia's prediction. I wasn't sure I'd want to hear what he had to say.

"Who's in the mood for beans?" Bertucci had asked, breaking the short spell Livvy had cast on me.

"When have I ever declined a visit to the Bean Pot, even if we already ate foods *a*, *b*, and *c*, and I have the coconut stuck in my teeth to prove it?" I took the next escalator as though it were nonmoving stairs, bounding up to get to the Bean Pot first.

"Escapades on Escalators require Emergency Protein," Bertucci said when he was behind me in line. Livvy had her arm snaked through his, but Bertucci's frame was awkward, and they looked like Dorothy and the Tin Man.

"Just remind me I have got to stay upwind of you both," Livvy said, but her face looked like she only ever wanted to be right next to us. I did not so much as dream of having my name in lights, more just having her there beside me to gaze at the marquee.

. . . .

Had I been so roped in by Lissa's looks? The tank tops that stuck to her skin that begged to be peeled off? Had Bertucci ever hooked up with her? Had we all wanted to bring her into the fold to make things easier? To disperse the weird triangle we'd become?

Probably I wanted Lissa to be more than she actually was. After the *Rashomon* movie, while Livvy'd ordered pizza, I told Bertucci about the bathroom session. "The thing about it is . . . she's the kind of girl who will come over to your house and give you a blowjob and then offer you brownies that she's just made. And not just regular brownies. Shit like s'more brownies or grasshopper brownies, which have these mint and dark chocolate chewy things." Bertucci fiddled with the plastic silverware—he ate pizza with a fork and knife—and regarded me with disgust. "My point is it's awesome but it's also kind of like, Really? That's what you want to be?"

Bertucci saw it: Lissa desperately trying to be part of us and failing. It had taken until now for me to admit it, when there wasn't really an *us* to be a part of anymore.

How sad it was to be only tangentially related to something that you wanted so much to be a part of. How pathetic it was to long so desperately for something. To have everything just out of reach.

I thought Bertucci would be with me when I went to the Circle lobby to open the package Lissa had handed me, but he was nowhere to be found. It was painful thinking about moving away from someone who knew me so well. Well enough that he could count on me forgetting the plan, reading every stupid inch of the *Brookville Baton*, and seeing the ad he'd placed. The fact that Lissa had also seen it and figured it out made me think that Bertucci had wanted her to show up. I didn't know if I'd ever make another friend like Bertucci. I guessed not.

I walked through the vacant back lobby past the never-inhabited snack bar, feeling almost normal. Then, right when I allowed myself that luxury, I did a double take. In the half-light, I craned my neck to see. Apprehension played at my fingers, wormed its way into my breathing.

I had to shift back and forth to make out the words, but it wasn't my imagination. That much I knew. Bertucci used to say I could be paranoid, and when I disagreed, he'd said, "In the words of the great David Foster Wallace, yes, but 'are you paranoid enough'?" Only I wasn't being paranoid. There, in the front of the sickly display of candy boxes, written in slanted script, were the words *I Know*.

I swore in my head and then aloud. Their prank had been stupid, the one on my bathroom mirror (though I didn't know if it was scary or hot that Olivia had been in there at some point), and truth be told it was lame by Bertucci's standards, but in the darkness of the movie house, it got to me. My own anxiety annoyed me. This in turn made me march over and wipe the words away with my sleeve.

Satisfied, I turned to go. A haunting thought occurred to me, and I was desperate to find Olivia, figure out what was in the package, and find a way out of the mess I'd created, but I also knew I had to turn around. Slowly, as though I was being watched, my lungs shook as I breathed and I pivoted.

There, where I'd swept the words away, were more words. The same words.

I know. I know.

I erased them again. They reappeared. I got rid of them faster and they rewrote themselves. Sweat and fear mixed on my skin.

What do you know? *I know.*

But what? *I know.*

It was like that game we had played in drama elective when we'd been assigned a phrase—*take the eggs* or *are you sure*—and you had to say it over and over again, changing your tone to convey a different emotion but never adding more words. It sounded dumb, but when I'd been paired with Livvy and she asked me for the fourteenth time *are you sure*, seeing the directness of her stare, I felt unhinged. I had excused myself with a bathroom pass, and by the time I was back the exercise was over.

Seeing *I know* in the coffee-colored light in the empty back lobby made me nauseated, the fear stinging the hairs on my neck, hairs that Livvy had once trimmed in her bathroom. I pictured her hands on my neck and remembered the way Bertucci had been the DJ, finding songs with the words *hair* or *cuts* or even the Molecules's cover of "Hirsute." It was like they were taking care of me somehow.

I heaved, puking onto the industrial carpet, then I backed away and fairly sprinted toward the main lobby, where I hoped Livvy was waiting for me—or at least hadn't taken off, done with the whole night, with me and my inability to express myself properly, with Bertucci's maniacal plans.

I reached the ticket booth out of breath, reeking of sick, wishing I'd thought to bring gum or breath mints even though as a rule I hate both gum and breath mints. Without realizing it, I'd gripped the package from Lissa so hard I'd torn part of it.

Light from the parking lot filtered into the room. I stood, hoping Livvy would show up or that Bertucci would tell me what he'd planned next. The black and white industrial clock ticked audibly, the ghosts of moviegoers past seemed to snake out from the ticket booth, all that pre-film anticipation sucked into the vacuum of time. I waited a full eight minutes before calling out.

"Liv—Olivia! I have something. We need to open this together!" No response. I tried again. "Lissa gave me something!"

Livvy stepped out from the shadows behind the large interior pillars. "An STD?"

"Yeah, gonorrhea."

"You can't even spell gonorrhea," Livvy said.

"Good thing she gave me a package instead, then," I said and waved the crinkled manila envelope at her.

She stepped closer to me. She'd taken off Bertucci's sweater and tied it around her waist, the arms of it long and flopping uselessly against her thighs. "Where is Lissa, anyway?"

"Gone," I told her. I tried to close the distance between us by moving to the front of the ticket booth where Livvy stood, but she came around back as I moved, making us only switch places. I leaned on the booth with both hands.

"Did she leave on her own, or was she pushed?" Olivia asked, referring to the paper I'd written, "Anna Karenina: Did She Fall, or Was She Pushed?" I'd gotten a B.

"I'm pretty sure she was pushed," I said. It wasn't convincing enough, and I knew I had to try and speak up. "I mean, I asked her to leave." I put the package on the ticket booth as though I were about to pay for admission, and Livvy plucked it with two fingers as one might a dirty jockstrap.

Olivia was the kind of person who takes forever to open presents, undoing the tape just so, saving the wrapping paper, basically being annoying as all fuck, so I was surprised when she ripped the padded manila envelope all the way.

She pulled out a piece of white paper, and instantly her face fell. She chewed on her lip. "Bertucci's writing." He had the kind of penmanship that guaranteed that, even if you lost touch for decades, the second a postcard arrived you'd know who it was from. All caps, each letter pointed as a spire. "Your basic instructional fare."

I took the note and read it aloud. "The best way out is always through." I coughed.

"I can't believe he asked her here," Livvy said, circling back into Lissa fallout.

"I know." I thought about touching Livvy's hair. "But I get it, sort of."

I could see Livvy acquiesce, her shoulders slumping. "Look, I know she's pretty. And objectively, she has the beginnings of a good person. At least, Bertucci thought so." Livvy paused. "Do you ever think maybe I tried to be friends with her—or you kept . . . whatevering with her—just to support that theory of his?"

"You mean, that she might be . . . one of us?"

Livvy nodded. "But squares collapse. Bertucci told me that."

"Bertucci said a lot of things."

Livvy sighed and said, "Fine," in a way that suggested anything but.

She tried to pull the package away from me, but I gripped it harder, reading aloud. *"In the rear of the main theater, you will find a balcony.* Like we don't know that? I was the one who showed him the balcony access."

"It's not a competition, for God's sake," Olivia snapped.

Everything's a competition. "Ok, sound system, blah blah

blah." I looked at her. "So, I guess we go?"

Olivia pulled a folded piece of paper out of the ripped package. "The CD. And another note." She held it out to face me. On the CD cover was a Post-it that read, *This should already be playing.*

"He knew she'd be late," I said, that sickening feeling building in my stomach. He always knew everything.

"Well, Lissa's always—" Olivia she shook her head. "Honestly, this whole thing is too weird to digest right now. Also . . . you smell gross."

"Thanks, Queen of Honest." I put my hand in front of my mouth and breathed, testing the nastiness. "I'm like an eight out of ten for gross." Olivia unzipped the small pocket at the front of her backpack. "You're like a CIA agent or something with all your shit in there," I told her.

"I hardly think spearmint gum and a wet wipe qualifies as covert special agent gear." She held out a piece of gum and I accepted it, the mint finally covering the sour taste on my tongue. Livvy looked out at the rain-wet glass, the eeriness almost suffocating us, and pointed to the windows. "Even my car headlights look sinister."

I nodded. "Should we . . ." I didn't complete the sentence because Olivia turned to glare at me, her eyes like the car's headlights, half-lidded and suspicious.

"You don't get to leave," she said, her hands tugging at her hair in frustration. "Don't you see that now?"

She was so authoritative that I found it grating. "I'm not trapped here!" I clenched my hands into useless little fists. "There's nothing to say I can't walk out that door and be home with a cup of tea in hand in under an hour."

"You don't drink tea."

I raised my eyebrows at her. "There's nothing keeping me here."

Her face flushed, her eyes wide as though I'd slapped her.

Livvy

"You know what your problem is?" I shouted at Codman. The words pushed out of my throat and flew at him like insistent crows, black and angry. "You're the son of two shrinks who can't express himself. God forbid you see this thing through, right? How horrible for you NOT to be able to bail. Just take off before you've had to see the point of the evening. Just leave it for Livvy, she'll deal with it. Isn't that your usual plan?"

Codman put his hands out from the ticket booth, his face serious. "You have no idea what I've been through, so I'm not sure you're qualified to comment on *my* night."

"Oh, give me a break," I said. "You don't think I know what you've been through? I'm like the only other person on this planet who knows."

Quickly, before Codman could stop me, I grabbed the package, sprinting away before he could object. Possibly I knew he wouldn't, and I was saving myself from further humiliation.

I got as far as the women's bathroom when I realized I'd left the CD and grabbed only the empty envelope. I let it go onto the floor, and then thought better of it. I crouched down, about to grab the paper.

On my knees, I heard it.

A cry.

A baby?

My mind raced. Had Bertucci stolen a human baby and left it in a deserted movie theater for us to find? I shook my head but knew it wasn't entirely out of the realm of possibility. That's how far Bertucci could go. He could have hacked into the Brookville General Hospital system and figured out how to gain access to the labor and delivery ward and faked an ID and—the next cry made my imagination stop.

It was high pitched and unrelenting and coming from a door near the women's bathroom. It was a door I'd never noticed on our regular movie outings, but this night was bound to do that, to show us things we'd previously ignored or tried not to think about.

I had no choice but to open the door. I did, but the space was completely lightless and the terror registered immediately. I could have yelled over my shoulder for Codman. I could have yelled out to Bertucci, angry and confused about why he'd done this, what he expected of me.

But I didn't. I just stood there, my breath coming fast, echoing because I knew I'd follow the crying, knew I'd take stairs and see what was there.

Codman

Olivia took off, leaving me to deal with the fallout. Who could blame her? I sort of owed her one on that front. She wasn't, by nature, a deserter. She was the one who lingered after the funeral. I took off as soon as I could, heaving up the cold cuts I'd plucked from the deli trays on Bertucci's kitchen counter. Livvy had a black piece of torn fabric pinned to her shirt. She saw me eying her, and for once it wasn't her breasts I was stuck on. "Kriah," she told me, scrubbing a dish that was already clean, just to be doing something. "You tear a piece of clothing or ribbon. Leave it to the Jews to know how to mourn." Had she been waiting for me to do the same? Express my grief and anger and fucking loss by ripping my shirt?

I knew she'd stay and clean up, that somehow she made it okay for me to leave in my unripped suit, like even my mourning was defective. Livvy could tough it out, could wait and hang on. She waited for Bertucci after college classes sometimes or stuck around at Bertucci's, lingering to make sure everything was tucked back in place. She was a stayer.

Olivia had plodded through countless baseball practices when my car was totaled, waiting just so she could give me a ride. Had I thanked her? Probably. But not enough. Possibly I was pissed at Bertucci—he'd been the one to wreck the car in the first place.

I'd taken the blame for that one, and Bertucci had never repaid me.

He was a solid driver, careful despite being an adrenaline junky.

"I wouldn't lend that guy your shoes, let alone your car," my stepbrother Dan had told me.

"His feet are way bigger than mine," I'd answered just to piss him off. Dan was a local cop who delighted in checking up on me or weighing in on his Brookville predictions—who was a hop, a skip, and a jump away from being a felon, who was most likely to shoplift.

"He's not borrowing it for long," I'd told Dan as I lobbed my keys to Bertucci. It was almost early spring. He felt like a road trip, he'd said, another one of his elaborate ideas only this time I wasn't invited. Not that he'd said as much but there was something in his voice that let me know not to ask.

"I'll have her back safe and sound ASAP," he'd said and slid into the driver's seat, the window rolled down even though it was March. He idled in the driveway. "What, you're gonna watch me go?"

I'd turned around, as if Bertucci taking off out of my driveway in my own shitty car that I'd saved for and bought only that fall was too personal for me to see.

Of course, the car never made it back. Dan called the house, all authoritative and serious. "There's been an accident."

My dad—Dan's biological father—stood up calmly from the dinner table and motioned for me to come to the phone. The pasta I'd eaten threatened to come up as I reached for the receiver. I expected Dan to launch into details about a crash, Bertucci in critical condition at Brookville General, casualties. But it was Bertucci's voice on the line.

"Hey, there, friend. Let me tell you a story. . . ."

It was idiotic, really. He'd found a discarded GPS at the junkyard. "They'd just left it in the car to rot."

"That's what you were doing? Driving my car to visit dead cars at Smitty's?" I'd only been to Smitty's once, with Bertucci's father right after we'd become friends. Before his drinking sort of took over, Bertucci's dad had a penchant for fixing things, and we'd gone in search of some obscure engine part on the way to pick up a pizza. It was a fun day mainly because going to a dump was nothing my parents would have done for kicks, but by the end of it, when his dad refused to give up searching and the light was gone and we were cold and hungry, I had no desire to be there or to go back to Bertucci's. I just wanted to bail. The sun had set on the half-beat cars, a few of them burned out, most stripped of useable parts. The newer ones were dropped right on top of the older ones as if to claim they were better, though I guessed they'd end up just like the junk underneath, forgotten about and skeletal.

"I was not planning a Smitty's run, though I do enjoy a car-cass. Hah. Anyway, I happened to find a GPS, and I fixed it. Mostly. I had it speak Russian to me."

"That's brilliant," I said, "except for the fact that you don't speak Russian."

"Yeah, but, I mean, how hard could it be, right?"

"Uh, yeah."

"I was like a deranged tourist. And, well, to sum it up because your cop brother is giving me looks here, I wound up in the river." He breathed deeply. "Well, not in it. Near it."

"But you're okay?" I asked. I wanted to ask about my car, but it seemed callous. At the same time, I was pissed at him.

It was like he knew what would happen but did it anyway. Bertucci was emotional caffeine—semi-necessary for functioning but possibly hazardous for me in the long run.

"I'll pay you back," Bertucci said, and his voice was solid. He meant it.

My father grabbed the phone from me, spoke to Dan, and hung up. "You realize this is not good, Alex," he told me. I nodded. He was concerned about Bertucci, about my direction in life, about college acceptances that had yet to arrive, about my car that was crumpled at the bottom of Lowell Bridge.

"I'll fix it," I said.

My father shook his head and made eye conversation with my mom. "I don't think you can."

I stood there in the Circle's disintegrating lobby without Livvy, without Bertucci, without my car, and felt the night closing in around me, tension welling up in my stomach and my shoulders. My father had been right. I couldn't fix it. But I wasn't ready to give up, either.

Livvy

Taking deep breaths, I slid my pack off my back and propped open the heavy door—not that this provided much light, but at least would let me know how to escape.

The cry intensified.

"Hello?" I asked, though I realized an infant wouldn't answer.

Wahhh. Rahhh.

I took a few steps in, wishing I wasn't alone, terror scratching at my throat. "Bertucci?" I said. It was possible he was nearby, though as I said his name I realized I was angry. He'd had this idea that we could all be better, better versions of ourselves, which I sort of hoped was true. I didn't want to shed my entire being the way some girls did, forgetting that only the year before they had opinions, dressed however they wanted to, and weren't meshed into a crowd. But at the same time I never knew with Bertucci. And what if I wanted to hold onto things?

His ideas teetered between amazing and crazy, and even though I had worried about him, about what he'd do next year without Codman to do a reality check and me to get him to take a deep breath, I went along with a lot of the plans because they were fun. And they pushed me in ways I probably never would have been pushed. It wasn't just roller coasters I didn't like, but being unprepared, changing plans, sudden anything, really. So when Bertucci would detour us out of the blue it frightened me, but it was also exhilarating, like having limbs I didn't know I had, a smile I hadn't seen, or courage I never had to test before.

I stood half-enveloped in shadows, one foot still anchored in the lobby, knowing I needed to rescue whatever was by the stairs. Saliva caught in my throat and I coughed. The echo of my own voice made me flinch. I knew I would go; I just waited for a push of some kind, the same kind of push I'd had by the roller coaster with Codman and Bertucci, the same nudge he'd given me on the Day of the Meters.

I was pretty sure I'd be able to tell the Day of the Meters story happily one day, as a memory composed entirely of simple, youthful joy. But for now, I had to admit that looking back was complicated. I could see the memory begin to unfold, to unspool, to come apart like an expertly sliced onion, but before I could even allow myself to consider what any of the fucking layers meant and whether any of them wouldn't bring me more tears, I heard another pounding.

"Lissa?" I asked, even though I doubted she'd come back. Part of me wanted her to get the fuck out of the Circle, out of our lives, go off to her banal future and never look back. But part of me needed her to remember, like somehow the more people who held on to this part of our lives, the more it mattered. The noise continued. This time, the slamming wasn't the side door but the front window.

I stood there, torn between the crying noise and the pounding, unsure which way to move. Finally, I went with the pounding, jogging over to the window, furrowing my brow as I tried to see who was out there. At the side door, I yelled to the front.

"Over here! This way!" I waited. In a minute, a guy with a red baseball cap appeared.

"I have your order," he said.

My mouth hung open. "Who called you?" I stared at his hat. A Slice from the Slice.

He shrugged. "I don't take the names, I just bring the orders." He checked his rain-damp receipt. "Double mushroom?" He held the paper bag out to me, steam escaping from the boxes inside. I could smell the melted cheese.

I swallowed. "How much do I owe you?" I asked.

"Nothing," he said. "It's all taken care of. You know, free calzone to each Brookville grad?"

I took the bag and watched him leave. He must deliver food to all kinds of crazy scenes, I figured, if he didn't comment on this location. Then again, maybe he just didn't care. I leaned back on the white plaster interior column near the ticket booth and slid down, the bag on my lap. The calzone was perfect—crisp on the edges but gooey with melted cheese in the middle. Just like the double mushroom we always ordered. After wiping the oil on my jeans, I texted. *Thanks, Bertucci! Calzones r here!*

He'd taken care of everything, I thought.

Almost everything.

As I ate, I thought back to the Day of the Meters, wishing he were with me so we could reminisce together.

"You realize, of course, people will think you've come unhinged," Codman had told Bertucci as we stood outside of the used bookstore on Main and Brook. I'd wondered why people had sold their books—were they saving money? Had they cleaned house and gotten rid of stories they no longer needed? What about the birthday inscriptions, the valentines from old loves?

"Did you seriously think we were just out for a walk through town?" Bertucci asked. He'd worn green army pants, the kind with myriad pockets of various sizes. Each one bulged and made him look as though he had some terrible disease.

I flinched when Codman used the word *unhinged* because it was a word I thought about in relation to Bertucci but never brought up for fear of how he'd react. Either he'd deny it and be pissed at me or agree and be sad, and neither of those options seemed like the way to go.

"You have a sort of Robin Hood complex," I had said as I watched Bertucci sling his arm around a parking meter as though it were a friend of some kind.

Codman bent down to tie the laces on his Golas, the English indoor soccer shoes he eventually bought five stores after the incident at Ski 'n' Golf. They had fluorescent orange stripes on the sides that glowed even brighter in the early summer light.

"Can you believe this is our last June together?" Bertucci asked. We had only a couple of weeks left of junior year.

I had frowned, eager to disprove his statement. "Just because we graduate next year doesn't mean we won't be together in some way, shape, or form."

The bookstore's awning unfurled with a mechanical whir, and someone unlocked the door from inside. "Do I have time to poke around?" I asked.

Bertucci shook his head. "No. Time is of the essence here."

Codman sighed. "Well, this essence better involve food at some point." He paused. "And a bathroom."

"That's it," I told Codman. "We're all chipping in and buying you your very own porta-potty for your birthday this year."

"Don't get me anything," Bertucci said. "Just continue these good deeds that we are about to put forth into the universe." He patted his full pockets.

"Just how long are we waiting here, anyway?" Codman asked.

Bertucci didn't answer, but I followed his gaze across the street. The church steeple rose above the buildings, reaching high as though trying to puncture the white-blue sky. There was a huge clock on the face of the church, but I doubted Bertucci could see the Roman numerals from where we were.

Codman started humming "Phantom Limb," and I started singing even though I never knew exactly what the lyrics were due to the fact that the Shins were hard-core mumblers.

And then, the minute the clock began to sound, we all stood at attention. Whether we knew it or not then, we took Bertucci's ideas seriously, almost reverently. *Bong. Bong.* Eight of them.

"Nine," Bertucci said. "Go!"

"The key is to make sure no one has those minutes where they're searching for change, or wondering if their meter is going to expire while they're in getting dog food or at the ATM," Bertucci told us. He was out of breath, already starting to sweat, the dark spots freckling his red T-shirt.

Armed with parking cards, quarters, dimes, and just enough nickels for the older meters by the library, the three of us worked like synchronized swimmers, filling meters, leaving the photocopied note on the windshield, and dashing up side streets to follow Bertucci's hand-drawn map he'd made the night before, while Codman was at his house presumably asleep and I was very much not asleep due to Bertucci's numerous texts reporting his progress.

He'd done his research with the town's layout but not where the meters were or how they varied by rate or credit card or Brookville parking pass. Plus, we all knew that the first Saturday in June was the busiest shopping day; stores had their sidewalk sales, the church bake sale kept families coming in droves until every last Krispy Treat and poorly-constructed M&M cookie was sold. Nine hours of work.

"I hope this pays off," I told Codman as he systematically pinched coins from a bag Bertucci had given him and pressed them into twin meters.

"I thought we were just doing this to be nice, not for profit," Codman said.

"Ah, Codman, my young friend," Bertucci had said, "Don't you know by now everything has a price?"

"But not necessarily," Codman said. "Read the note."

"I did," I said. "At three in the morning."

"The key is to turn off your phone, Olivia," Codman told me. "He can't get to you if you don't have it on."

Bertucci coughed. "Ahem. I am right here. And also? I can get to you both at all times. I'll haunt you when I'm gone. Anyway, Liv, you only read the early draft."

He handed me one of the bright yellow fliers he'd been leaving under windshield wipers.

It's your lucky day. No, really!
Please forgive our trespasses! We are but poor
and innocent youths trying to help you and to help
ourselves at the same time.
We have fed your meter and will continue to do so all day!
You might choose just to see me as an angel, someone who
is looking out for you and your best interests.
Or you might decide that our services are worth
something to you. If this is the case, please
leave your donation in the lockbox between _____
and _____.

"Please tell me the blanks are intentional," I said.

"That's my job—what do you think I've been doing?" Codman displayed his marker-stained left hand.

"The lockboxes are equidistant and—" Bertucci started, but I cut him off.

"You have a dumb typo," I said. "Right here. 'We have fed,' et cetera. 'We' this and 'we' that, but then it says 'me.'"

"No, you're wrong," Bertucci insisted, anxious to keep moving.

I shoved it too close to his face, and he batted it away. *"You might see me as an angel,"* I read.

Bertucci looked genuinely surprised and studied a few copies before accepting it. "Just cross it off."

"Just ignore it," Codman said. "No one'll notice."

"Just black it out," Bertucci insisted and handed me a Sharpie from the depths of one of his pockets.

From Elm to Main, zigzagging from the drugstore's back exit to the supermarket, we ran, filling meters and leaving notes, sometimes being met by drivers about to put money in or who'd just driven up. They were thrilled. Grateful. Sometimes annoyed only because they were confused.

"Is this a ploy to get me to pay you double?" one guy in a suit asked outside the dry cleaners. We explained. He looked skeptical. Bertucci stepped in.

"Sir, I can assure you there is no ill will here," Bertucci said. I loved his language. He appeared grown up, older sometimes than actual grown-ups. "You can decide to pay or not. There's no judgment here."

"So this is just an act of goodwill?" the suit guy asked.

"Exactly," Bertucci said, and we moved on. Later, he would check each of the sixteen lockboxes he'd left between buildings or the ground. I had asked him if he was concerned about someone stealing them—they weren't bolted down or secured in any way—but Bertucci shrugged and told me he had this idea that people would overlook them.

I had nodded. "At Passover my dad used to hide the afikomen—that's the matzo for those non-Jews among us,"

I said. "And he'd sometimes put it right on the mantel, displayed like artwork."

"And you didn't notice, did you?" Bertucci asked. He craned his body across an SUV to stick a flier under the wiper. "No, that's the thing," he went on. "People just go about their days not really noticing. It is my prediction that the boxes will contain the funds for college apps or what-have-you and then some, and that they will be intact, unopened, and not tampered with at the six o'clock bell."

And he was right. No one bothered to notice. Or they did—because they put coins or dollar bills, even a twenty— inside the lockboxes, but they didn't steal anything. Codman thought this was because people are good at heart, but Bertucci insisted that it was because those involved either donated funds or didn't, and those not involved were too focused elsewhere to even see the box right in front of them.

The sun was slipping down behind the spire, still high enough that I was hot, but the day was fading, and I felt the sting of what Bertucci had said earlier—this was our last first Saturday in June together. It was difficult not to do the countdown to the end of life as we knew it.

The outdoor lawn selection at the hardware store was set up like a mock barbecue, and the three of us collapsed into the mesh chairs. "Pass the ketchup," Codman said, and I mimed chucking the bottle at him while Bertucci examined the contents of the boxes.

"Looky here—a note back." He unfolded it and read, "I have to leave my therapy sessions in the middle to feed the fifteen-minute meter. This causes me great anxiety, which is why I am in therapy in the first place. This ten-dollar bill is my gratitude. I hate to bother you, but would you mind doing this again every other Saturday morning from 10:00 to 10:50? I would be most grateful. You *are* an angel!" Bertucci looked smug. Codman rolled his eyes.

"Guess you have to say no, huh?" I'd asked.

Bertucci had looked at me with a wrinkled forehead. "No. I will absolutely do this until further notice."

I had to leave for tennis practice and go right from there to Marta's, and I felt left out already, as though worlds of events and conversation would take place in my absence. Bertucci read my mind. "Codman, we must say nothing of import while Livvy is off with her other friends."

Codman drew an X on his chest and I followed his finger with my eyes. "I promise. Nothing. We'll be boring paralyzed mimes."

"Band name!" Bertucci said. "Boring Paralyzed Mimes. Live from Des Moines!"

"BPM. College band with one hit that crosses the mellow musings of Ryan Adams with Icelandic instrumental," I quipped.

Codman grinned at me, his face golden in the fading light.

I began to walk away and Bertucci used his hands as a megaphone. "Album title: *Need I Say More?*"

I wound my way through the jammed parking lot, the meters now expiring and flicking to red like matching metronomes. I stretched my arms high above my head out of habit. I looked back, and Codman was doing the same thing, not because he saw me doing it but because he'd adopted the stretch as his own. It's a shoulder-opener for serves and lobs.

It was comforting, seeing parts of yourself in other people. Bertucci showed up in Codman, or traits of mine were displayed—when Codman used the words *in fact*, words that he'd mocked me for early in our friendship that now were second nature to him. I knew no matter how much distance we'd have between us after graduation, I would always use the word *myriad* and find foreign rap songs cool, wisps of Bertucci that had seeped into my life and that I didn't even need to hold onto to keep. They were just there.

I sometimes wished I'd been aware of adopting those ticks, the way Codman stretched two-syllable words into three—*he-lo-oo!* But I think I knew that's not the way things happened—you just woke up one day and had that habit, said those words that way or paused as though you were the one who originated it. You didn't know how or why someone had become part of you, it just was that way.

Even though I didn't bring it up, I knew things would have to change between us. That they would even if I didn't want them to.

"We're a triangle," I'd said to Bertucci one winter afternoon at Lady Foot Locker. He was reshelving all the shoes no one had wanted, checking to make sure both were in the box, that the box was labeled correctly, and that there was room on the shelf. I felt stupid for saying it, aware suddenly of how my voice sounded in the people-less store. I also knew that if Codman were there I never would have said it. It was possible I didn't want to be a triangle with Codman. Just a pair. No shape at all. Bertucci flipped a pair of ugly sport flip-flops around and slapped the cover on the box. "J. Wetzel remarked that triangle geometry has more miracles per square meter than any other area of mathematics."

"Should I ask who J. Wetzel is?"

"You should think about properties of the triangle," Bertucci said and on my arm sketched $a^2 + b^2 = c^2$.

"You're giving me the Pythagorean theory as arm graffiti?"

"That's us," he said and went back to shelving. "Pythagorean triple."

Outside the store, I had shielded my eyes from the glare. I could see Bertucci pick his hand up from the table, hardly a wave, but enough of one so I knew he directed it at me.

. . . .

At the Circle, I thought about Bertucci's hands, how still they were. No matter how fast he spoke or how much his mind raced, his hands were calm. Large and still. I took a few more steps inside the dark stairway, stepped away from the safety of the door, concentrating on my breathing as the cries reverberated from the stairwell. *Rarrr. Ennnnh.*

With every baby cry, my panic grew, my heart responding exactly the way I'd learned in Bio. We are designed to rescue, designed to need to go to the cry.

The darkness closed up around me, and I could not see my hands or feet or where I stepped. I could only hear the cry.

It wasn't an infant. It was a cat.

If roller coasters topped of the list of things I loathed and mushy French toast came second, then cats would be third. But I found myself doing that instinctive cat kissy noise to get the thing to come over. I couldn't get my bearings in the blackness, and I didn't turn around for fear of getting so disoriented I'd be stuck in the bowels of the cinema forever.

"You can't stay in here," I said, probably to myself as well as the cat. How long could a cat last in a basement? Could it see the pipes or whatever else was down there? Were there rogue mice on which it could live?

After several minutes of embarrassing kissing noises, I felt a small swish of air and then a lithe body swirling around my ankles.

"Please be a cat and not an opossum," I told it. I backed up and the animal followed me, stepping onto my backpack and then out the door. It looked up at me, its eyes the same peculiar shade of gray as Bertucci's. "Oh, are you Bertucci?" I asked. The cat tilted its head as though it understood, and this time a little bell—the kind that suggested fairies or elves—rang out.

I did not enjoy cat purrs or their arched backs or their fur, soft as it may be, but I reached down, and there on the cat's neck was a tiny bell attached to a tiny placard. I squinted to read it but couldn't. I sighed and shook my head, slung my pack on my back, and gathered the animal into my arms.

"Look what the cat dragged in," I said aloud for Codman's benefit when I was back in the lobby, the parking lot's light illuminating the cat's tabby coat. It was lean and had white paws, which I supposed would be cute for those prone to thinking such things. I looked around. Codman wasn't there.

My heart sank.

For the first time, I thought about graduation, how it was only a handful of hours away. Our caps and gowns would be delivered soon, stacked in the gym by the rising seniors, as was tradition. Bertucci had talked about going naked under his gown. Codman had talked about not showing up. I hadn't thought much about the ceremony, more about what we'd do after. After the funeral, the Millennium Gold just sat there glinting in the sun and it had hit me that all that scurrying around making sure there were platters of cold cuts back at Bertucci's for people to pick at while they mourned, all the discarded programs, all of that was just busy work. All stuff that could be cleaned up. It was the stuff we weren't saying, weren't addressing, that couldn't be swept away in the dustbin. I could picture the black graduation gowns all puddled onto the gym floor as though we were shadows or people who had melted.

Meow. Now the cat sounded like a cat. How could I have thought it was a baby? I studied the placard. It was one of those first-day-of-school name tags we'd all had to wear for the entire first week of freshman year.

"Hi! My name is SCHRÖDINGER."

Bertucci's writing had the name in all caps.

"Schrödinger?" I asked. "What the hell kind of name is Schrödinger?"

Bertucci

Livvy did sometimes lie, that I knew. Mainly to herself about Codman. But also about me, probably. Definitely about her knowledge of quantum physics—a course I'd taken at the college and that she'd asked me to tell her about nearly word for word, fascinated.

She had cooked dinner—crispy roasted chicken with these shredded potato things and a bunch of vegetables I could identify only because Codman's mom grew them in her garden, and I'd taken to sleeping at their house a lot at that time, even when Codman was off looking at schools. It wasn't just because Bee had died but also because I felt slightly better outside my own house, sort of like stepping outside my skin. Codman's house was the opposite of Livvy's. Where Livvy's was clean to the point of looking almost sterile—objects from their travels displayed in militaristic order on the built-in shelves, the thermostat always a few degrees too cold—Codman's was cluttered with stacks of mail, wooden sculptures of families, tattered quilts thrown on the back of a chair and never folded, medicine cabinets with outdated bottles, the fridge stocked with casseroles and leftovers and kale or chard from the garden.

I wasn't the only one of us who felt an affinity for other people's homes. Despite the cleanliness and organic crackers at her place, Olivia always seemed relieved when she came over to my house. Like she had freedom there. We never had fresh fruit and the furniture had not been updated and the main work of art was my father's empties, but she'd enter as though this was her home. She cleaned as though she could actually make a difference in the kitchen and always arrived with something for my mom: a scented candle or lotion her parents had brought back from some fancy conference hotel or homemade bean dip and celery that would wither by week's end.

But I'd gone to Olivia's that night. Maybe she'd given up coming to my house or didn't want to show up at Codman's. Her room had dark hardwood floors. We sat there, my textbooks and binder opened to show her objective collapse theories. Olivia had flipped through the pages, making fun of me yet again for taking written notes instead of typed. "I mean, what happens if you lose them?"

"How do I lose them?" I asked.

She shrugged. "I don't know. There's a fire."

"If there's a fire, my notes are the least of my worries."

She laughed. "Fair enough." She chewed her upper lip. "If it's . . . if it's because you don't have a laptop, we have an extra . . . " Her face had apology written on it.

"I'm good. I actually like the writing. It sort of helps get the info to stay." I pointed to my temple like that's where the quantum physics file was stored.

We'd stayed there on the floor that Thursday night, me telling her all about my class, all about Schrödinger's equation and his cat as if it was just another night in the life of us. Nothing to look at, folks; just move along. Livvy had her head in her hands at one point like we were already apart from each other as we'd all probably imagined it. I know I had.

I'd been wearing the same gray T-shirt with the dot, and she'd pressed her finger into the dot saying what was printed on it. "You are here." She repeated it.

"Always," I said.

My sweater had been on the floor of her room, and she'd slipped it on. "Why is it always so cold in my house?"

"Because you need to borrow my sweater," I'd said. "Keep it."

Livvy. I see her now as I did then, in my sweater. In a category all by herself:

Kingdom of females

Phylum of attractive girls

Class of upper—or at least a class beyond my split-level cul-de-sac hyphenated world

Order of girls who probably were in love with Codman

Family of large-breasted ladies who also have brains and thus are even more likely to break my heart

Genus of the able

Species totally unlike my own and yet so familiar it made me fold in on myself when I'd see her walk down the corridors, always at the edges, not like she was avoiding the throngs of guys in their football uniforms or lemming girls in whatever the go-to outfit was then, but more like she'd figured out that the edges of the halls, of life maybe, were the coolest parts.

It was also possible I just didn't know enough girls to make a generalization.

Codman showed up much later but by then we'd put the notes away and were listening to music and playing dirty phonetic Scrabble. I was itching to go.

Probably Olivia remembered what I'd told her about Schrödinger and all that but—as with the case of so much science and theory—hadn't figured out the practical implications of it.

Or she had, but was lying.

Codman

To be fair, I come from a long line of cowards. My father asked my mother to marry him through a mutual friend. My sister had been the first and only person to withdraw from her valedictorian post, her fear of public speaking too intense. Dan became a cop because he was terrified of them and of laws, guns, and jail. I could handle dares and exactly two tallboys before barfing and most of Bertucci's big ideas, but that spring he'd become a burden. On the escalators, I was on high alert. Disaster loomed everywhere.

Or maybe I'd had fun and was only putting those feelings on my memories as my therapist suggested. Maybe in hindsight everything was scary, scary because it seemed each action solidified the outcome of what had actually happened. Maybe senior spring had just been plain old fun, but in the Circle it didn't feel that way.

I gave up trying to find Olivia, and when I realized she'd left the CD and the note, I fought the urge to throw up again and instead bucked the trend of cowardice. I didn't want to be the guy who left. The guy who couldn't deal—perpetually—and Livvy's words filled my pockets, making me feel heavy. It had been a mistake to leave her back at Bertucci's that afternoon, to basically go into hiding the past few weeks, to run when I should have planted myself next to her. The thought of such distance between us made my chest heavy.

Had it really only been six months since the three of us had fallen asleep on her bed? Since *Rashomon*? Only weeks since Memorial Day? The days and weeks expanded and then instantly contracted the more I tried to hold on to them. Is that what we were supposed to do, revisit and retell so that there wasn't a clear definition between past and present?

In spring, we'd all gone to Livvy's for Passover. Bertucci, ever the kiss ass, sat methodically folding napkins for the table while I was with Livvy in her room.

"What are you doing?" I'd asked her even though it was obvious.

"Watering a plant, O Observant One." she said. We were in a phase of calling each other "O ___ One." O Horny One, O Revolutionary War–Inspired One, O Plump-Gutted One (this last Bertucci had so called me because I'd torn a ligament in my foot running after him on one of his epic night jogs and thus hadn't been running and had been eating Lissa's after-school treats—all bar-shaped).

"But you're way invested in that fern."

"It's aloe, fuckling."

"Sorry, O Plant-Genius One."

Livvy turned to me, her hair over part of her face. I'd fought the urge to tuck it behind her ear—I could have, but what would that mean?

"There's this thing, zakhor," she'd said. "It's like for Jews there's this sort of collective memory. You should know this, O Half-Chosen One."

"Like Holocaust Remembrance Day?" I asked.

Did I know she was Jewish? Sure. Did I fully get it? Not really. I was half, but half meant sort of nothing. It just wasn't something I had fully integrated into the person I knew Livvy to be. Like we all had these mini worlds we belonged to—Bertucci's math and chess, how my brother and I had taken automotive classes for six years and both of us could rebuild a V-6 but I didn't walk around saying so. All these pockets existed in people, and you had to connect them or at least remember them when you were trying to get to know, really know, someone.

"You were here for Rosh Hashana," Livvy said. I nodded, but she explained anyway, because she knew me well enough to know I might not actually have paid attention. "The Jewish New Year? You know, that big dinner a couple years ago when my grandmother got drunk and said the same toast twice and my mom tried to distract everyone by forcing kugel on them." I nodded and she translated. "Noodle pudding. Kugel."

"Oh yeah, that shit's the best. Seriously." I remembered sitting next to her, my thigh pressing into hers, hers pressing back, and how we did nothing about it later. "With the little plump raisins and the crushed cornflakes . . ."

"So that's a new beginning," Livvy said. "And Yom Kippur's the day of atonement, where you think of the year that's gone by and what you wish . . ." She paused and bit her upper lip. "What you wish you'd done differently. Better." She'd plucked a few stray brown leaves from the plant in front of her. "My grandmother died after that meal. Not, like, right away, but soon." Livvy touched the aloe plant. "She—Grandma Ruth—always kept aloe on the windowsill near the stove. Good for burns."

I touched the pointy leaf, which was really an excuse to get my hand near Livvy's.

"Jewish people," Livvy said to me, but I thought maybe she meant us too, "have this collective memory. And it flows through all the meals, the rituals, the candle lighting at Chanukah . . ."

"I love a latke," I said. Bertucci and I had eaten fourteen potato pancakes each—ill-advised, yes, but delicious—tucked in Livvy's well-organized pantry during her parent's annual Who-Can-Spell-Chanukah Party.

"So zakhor, remember, O Brilliant One, is in the Hebrew bible, but Jews in general are told not to forget." She broke off a piece of aloe, and we'd watched drops ooze from the stem. She rubbed it on my wrist. "*Zakhor* is an active word, so you go on remembering, telling stories of the people who have died, ritualizing them, your memories, and history, so nothing is really dead." She slid her fingers on my inner wrist. "As long as you're talking and remembering, the person—or the event—is still there with you."

I wanted to cry, listening to her, the cadence of her voice, how she'd so obviously thought about this and told me. But what I said was, "So you're telling me you have Jewish plants?"

Which is right when we turned and noticed Bertucci, who'd slinked into the doorway, quiet but hearing, and I felt like such a dick. Why couldn't I have held her hands and said, I understand. Your grandmother is the plant. So you have to take care of it, and you have to tell me about her drunk toast because on some level it's what keeps her from being obsolete. But I'd said nothing.

"Reshaped memories," Bertucci had said, which covered my assholic reaction and also made him saintly. Of course he'd heard. Of course he'd gotten it, knew what to say. "Like now, at Passover," he'd said while Livvy pressed the dirt into the pot, tried to angle it in the sun on the windowsill even though it was late afternoon and getting dark. "One of the central dictums of the Seder: in each and every generation, let each person regard him- or herself as though they had emerged from Egypt."

Livvy nodded, looking at Bertucci the way she had the aloe. "It enforces the fusion of past and present. It's how you get a collective memory."

"Zakhor," I'd said, but by then they weren't listening, only I was.

Bertucci surveyed the room—the two of us, the plants. "Like Doctor Who."

Livvy frowned. "What?"

Bertucci took up the entire doorframe, his hands in the top corners as though supporting the thing. "'I'll be a story in your head, but that's okay, because we're all stories in the end.'" He paused. "Just make a good one, eh?'"

. . . .

My chest felt weighted with memory. I felt my wrist as though the aloe stick would still be there. When would that ease?

Heavy and scared as I trekked all alone to Theater 1.

The main theater was the original stage, back when the whole building was a single theater with movies accompanied by a live organist, the seats antiqued and not particularly comfortable. The management had tried for a retro-cool look, preserving the thick velvet curtain and the ornate metal wall decor, but had only succeeded in making the room look like a decrepit mental asylum.

As I approached the main door, I had to do a double take. I got to where I thought the entrance was, and there was a wall. Around the corner was another door, but when I got there, feeling along like I was trying to read braille, there was only more wall, more obsolete movie posters.

I remembered going to the anti-Oscars film fest the year before with Livvy and her friend, Marta. Bertucci had arrived halfway through, slipped into our row, and reached for popcorn like he'd been there all along. The Circle played the World's Worst Movies on Oscar day, colossal flops and laughable attempts that made the audience recite bad lines or howl with laughter.

"Let's move to the balcony," Bertucci had suggested.

"No way," Marta had said. She was Olivia's oldest friend, a fellow tennis player, very type A. "It's off-limits."

"Nothing's off-limits," Bertucci told her.

Olivia defended her friend. "Marta's right—we have good seats here."

Bertucci tried again but we didn't end up moving. "I'm always afraid I'll fall off," Marta whispered as the next movie started.

"Fair enough," Bertucci had said.

Now I paced the theater wondering what was wrong with me until it hit me. "Senior Doorway!" I said and began pounding the walls for space or for a hollow sound, anything that would suggest that the doorway was underneath and merely hidden. "You're repeating yourself, Bertucci! Sloppy."

But it wasn't sloppy. It took me a long time to find the seam, to wrestle the plywood piece from the wall in order to gain access to the theater. Inside, the theater's emergency lights were on but almost entirely faded, causing the already dilapidated room to look haunted.

Had we really sat there, laughing and eating popcorn at the anti-Oscars? Had we really worn costumes and done the *Princess Bride* Quote-Along, holding inflatable swords and chucking peanuts at the screen when the line called for it?

It was like everything that had come before was a different life that had happened to another person, only I was also aware that I was that person. Somewhere there was something that would connect that past and the present. My fingers squeezed the plastic CD cover hard enough that it snapped, creating a shard that sliced my hand. I winced and sucked the blood off, trying to muster the courage to take the hidden stairwell at the side of the theater.

I stepped onto the stairs, trying to ignore my anxiety. The sheer terror of being anywhere in the dark, not to mention in the dark alone, pulsed around me.

Why had I stepped away from Livvy again? What kept me from from holding her hand and pulling her up the dark stairwell with me? I stopped.

My palm stung. My legs felt both hollow and filled with concrete—unsteady but horribly weighted. I forced myself to go farther and opened the door. The first thing I saw was a stereo, all wired and, in case I was too blind to make it out in the half-light or too freaked out to function, there was an arrow and a note slapped on it. "CD goes here."

I did as I was instructed and pressed play, listening to the first few songs, which Bertucci had deftly edited into 30-second samples. They brought back memories of flinging the Frisbee back and forth across Bertucci's scrubby backyard. Rap in German, pop in French, Sinéad O'Connor ("Hottest bald chick ever," Bertucci had explained when he'd played her album *I Do Not Want What I Haven't Got* in full for us). Olivia had been into Elvis Costello; I could see her in the upstairs window looking adorable in a sundress, dancing, no doubt putting on an English accent. *Murder, pretending?* Now those lyrics weren't pop music but scary.

I skipped forward—breaking the rules of a mix as far as Bertucci was concerned—and found the Beatles. Good old reliable Beatles. I sat there, finding comfort in singing songs that I'd known forever, that my parents had played on Sundays while they read the paper. A song asked where did you go, and I tried to picture sitting at graduation, my butt on the hard folding chairs as they made speeches and handed out diplomas and people in the audience clutched their Kleenex. My mom would want to frame my diploma, and I'd probably let her, but it didn't mean that much. It was just paper. It couldn't possibly be the sum total of everything I'd done and experienced over the past four years. In fact, at this point, it seemed like a stupid marker.

I looked up and, with a start, saw Bertucci leaning against the projector wall, hand on top of it.

"Stop doing that," I said, my voice wobbly and light. "Stop freaking showing up and scaring the crap out of me."

He grinned and lip-synched, like a nonchalant, affable Nick Drake, all loose-limbed and graceful. Bertucci had perfect timing and terrible pitch and rarely sang out loud except in the shower. Livvy and I would sit there waiting for him sometimes, laughing at his tone-deaf version of "I'll Follow the Sun" or "Harvester of Sorrow" or whatever randomness appeared in his brain.

"Any thoughts about what I should say at graduation?" I asked him, though I knew Bertucci would give me nothing.

A couple of years before, I'd been stuck on my sophomore speech, the required five-minute talk each Brookville student had to give, and I'd begged him to help. He was the kind of guy who didn't write it, just ad-libbed a perfect five minutes on Simon and Garfunkel's song "The 59th Street Bridge Song (Feelin' Groovy)" as a philosophical statement. But he wouldn't give me ideas for topics or, once I'd chosen the Art of Contradiction (my Art of Contraception idea had been negged by my teacher), he didn't offer suggestions either.

Reductio ad absurdum. Reduction to the absurd. I'd spoken of my own experience with it, the old parent-child convo: Why'd you cheat? All my friends were cheating. So if all your friends jumped off a bridge you'd do that?

Bertucci kept staring at me, miming the song.

"My sophomore speech sucked," I said. "Everyone loved yours—you and your soundtrack." I paused. "Oh my God. I am so thick. That's what this is, right?" I pointed to the CD. "This is the soundtrack of tonight?"

I thought I could see Bertucci nod in the darkness, the way he always had, not a full nod, more of a head flick. "What am I supposed to say tomorrow?" I asked again and sighed.

I thought of Olivia, of asking her. Why was I so afraid of it? In that balcony, I became aware that telling Olivia meant telling myself. That's what made it so hard.

I was expected to make a speech at graduation, and I wondered if maybe I should talk about "Feelin' Groovy," the song that played right then. Probably not. Perhaps about how diplomas themselves are not eco-friendly. How probably tattoos are more appropriate. Not that I had any or wanted to get ink injected into my skin. But they were permanent and perhaps a better indicator of everything, a scar of some kind that would fade but never disappear.

Livvy

The music blasted so loud I figured the cops would show up any minute. I lived my life in constant fear I was doing something wrong, always second-guessing myself and my actions. That's how I felt about Codman and Bertucci. If I'd said something different to them, or opened up more, if I'd flung open some doors and closed others, would things be different?

The music kept coming, rolling over me in waves, and I could almost see Bertucci kneeling on the floor of Codman's room, flipping through the albums that Codman stored in old milk crates. There was an order to them, but I didn't know what it was. I was content to sit there not knowing, letting the guys pick songs or have them find the ones I wanted to hear. They both had an appreciation for vinyl. One I didn't share but didn't mind.

Bertucci, I realized, must have rigged up the entire sound system, coming to the Circle Lord knows how many times to set this up. Such preparation. Or maybe it was easier than I thought and Bertucci had connected a few wires, flipped a few switches, and presto—instant soundtrack.

I knew that's what it was from the second the notes piped out of the oversized white speakers that perched atop the metal beams near the ceiling.

This didn't mean I knew what to do.

In fact, I became convinced that leaving was the best option. Certainly I wasn't going to be able to talk to Bertucci about everything or tell Codman my real feelings in this context, so why stay?

Because I had showed up.

Because I could.

I felt rooted to the lobby, the cat coiled up on my belly as I sat on the floor eating my grainy bruised apple, waiting for a sign. How long had the cat lived here in the decrepit building? I pictured Bertucci bringing food. Had he checked on the cat regularly or left it to fend for itself? Cats could do that, I had heard, survive for long periods of time with very little to sustain them.

Not that I was big into signs, but I wanted something—anything that would give me direction.

The cat purred. "What's the matter? You don't like French pop music?" I asked as I hummed. I half-expected the cat to answer. Maybe Bertucci had rigged that too. But Schrödinger didn't answer. I looked at the tag. Schrödinger.

"Oh, Schrödinger! I get it! You're the cat!"

I had sat that night on my bedroom floor, trying to wrap my head around the complexities that spewed from Bertucci's mouth. He pointed to his physics textbook and his hand-written notes that I teased him about but secretly found charming.

Codman and I had planned to go to my parents' beach house the next morning, cutting class for my first time ever to beat the Memorial Day weekend traffic.

"Are you sure you don't want to come?" I'd asked Bertucci. Codman wasn't there, and I worried that he was having second thoughts about coming with me; that, like me, he could easily picture the two of us, hand in hand on the beach, sharing a room at night, the triangle broken.

There were so many reasons for loving Codman: the way my gut ached after he'd make me laugh; how he told me stuff he never told anyone else; how nice he was to his parents even though they drove him crazy with their need to talk, talk, talk about feelings and drive and motivation; and how kind they were to him even though he fundamentally let them down on a regular basis. How he looked when the sun caught the tips of his hair as he played Frisbee. How he knew I was watching but didn't make fun of me for that, he just gave a wink I could see even from far away. How he'd cut soccer practice—getting benched for that week's game—to bring me homemade banana bread when I was sick. Were there eggshells in a few bites? Yes, but still. Codman had a way of telling stories and putting his hand on my arm so firmly it felt like I was actually anchored to something. He was aware of his own faults, too, which was something else to love him for.

And yet I hated him for not showing that night, for that space on the floor beside me that should have contained Codman's jean-clad legs, his navy blue long-sleeved T-shirt pushed up to the elbows as he did when he was concentrating. But he wasn't there. It was me and Bertucci.

"Don't you want to join us?" I asked. "Road trip? Lobsters? Cookout? Beach?"

"Those are all good words," Bertucci said, though his face was stony. "But no. You young folks cut class and head out. I appreciate the invite—"

"You don't have to be invited," I said. Did he feel left out? Had I made it seem like a thing? Like it was a setup for me and Codman? Was it?

"I have plans of my own," Bertucci had said, and he didn't

sound wounded at all. Just matter-of-fact and monotone, the way he often did when he was in one of his depressive moods. He tapped the textbook in front of him.

Bertucci had gone through various equations, which made some sense though in a hazy way. Was I super interested in it all? Not really. A little, I guess. But he seemed so determined to have me get it, to know what he was explaining. His hands shook as he flipped the pages so I began doing it instead, which he interpreted as more interest on my part. Did I ask him why he was so nervous? No. And maybe I hated myself for that too.

"Erwin Schrödinger."

"Oh, you know I love an umlaut," I said, and Bertucci gave a smile that betrayed effort.

"So he's trying to demonstrate a sort of conflict between everything that quantum theory tells us—"

"Which is?" I tried to get Bertucci to look at me or to take a chip from the bowl of sour cream and onion triangles I'd dumped in there, but he refused. He hadn't been eating much of anything lately, and even though the organic baked potato snacks were hardly appetizing, I hoped he would at least feign interest in them. He'd hardly touched the dinner I'd worked hard to make. It had occurred to me that maybe I had roasted the vegetables and made extra potatoes and greens in the hopes that Codman would show up in time to eat them, being instantly won over by my incredible cooking skills.

"Quantum theory is the theoretical basis of modern physics that explains the nature and behavior of matter and energy on the atomic and subatomic level." Bertucci's gaze stayed on the text, but he seemed to slip away from me, from my room, from our conversation. I tapped his shoulder to bring him back. "What we are told about nature and behavior versus what we observe."

"So, what we see might be different than what we think we know?" I asked. The textbook had a silly sketch of a cat inside a three-dimensional box.

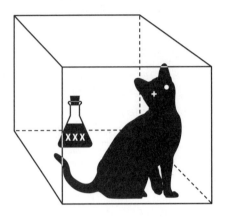

"You take a cat—a living cat. And you put it into a box—a metal one, let's say. And you also put in a vial of hydrocyanic acid."

"Why would we do this to the cat?" I asked, digging bits of chips out of my teeth with my tongue.

Bertucci rolled his eyes. "Because it's just the way it is." He looked at the door, probably wondering where Codman was, if he'd show up, if showing up then determined whether he'd come through on the night of the Circle. "Along with the cat and the acid, there's . . ." I reached out to take his shaking hand, quieting it with my own as he went on talking. "Anyway, it doesn't matter if you know what the acid properties are. You just need to understand that the cat's in there," he pointed to the box, "and a vial and a tiny bit of other shit that has the ability to decay."

I watched his face and tried to picture him explaining this to a class. His grant at UC–Berkeley involved being a TA and eventually giving lectures, and I knew he'd love it, crafting lesson plans, flirting with the hot physics undergrads if there were such a thing.

"Huh?" I cleared my throat. "I'm not trying to sound dumb, Bertucci. I just . . . what?"

He clapped his hands, the sound drawing attention to the stillness in my room. He was frustrated, his voice sharp, and it set me on edge. "Okay. If a single atom decays, it trips a mechanism which then breaks the vial and thus kills the cat."

"This is kind of a sick experiment. I can't believe this is the stuff you wrote about for your apps while I was busy talking about teaching tennis to the less fortunate."

Bertucci softened for a minute. "What would you write if you were applying now?"

I shrugged. "I don't know. Maybe how I want to go to Thailand. And work with kids and elephants?"

"You do know your way around a curry." He waited for more, like he knew I had it in me.

I took another chip. "I guess I'd write about your mom." I paused. "Is that so weird?" Bertucci shook his head. Bee had died a while before, but when I said her name or spoke of her, it felt like it had just happened hours ago. "I mean, not her exactly. But, you know, how I took care—we took care of her. I just . . . I feel like I can do that, you know?"

"You can," Bertucci said.

"So what happens with the cat?" I asked when Bertucci didn't say anything else.

"It's a theoretical experiment."

"Oh. So it's not like people are actually sitting there shoving a cat into a box to make a point?" I frowned. "Wait. What is the point?"

Bertucci stood up, leaving me on the floor feeling very small as he wandered around the room as though memorizing it, taking in the poster I had up, the framed photographs of me and Marta, me with Codman and Bertucci way back at the end of freshman year when I still had braces, my hair cut to my chin.

"It's in a box. It's a metal box with no holes. And you can't see in, so we can't know whether the cat is alive or dead. It's a superposition of states. Because you'd have to break open the box to know."

I sat there feeling that the floor was somehow buckling beneath me, that I was in over my head but had no clue why or how I'd gotten there. "The observation affects the outcome, so you don't have an outcome?"

Bertucci nodded. "According to quantum law, the cat is both alive and dead."

"Schrödinger's Cat," I said and reread the text as though this time I'd fully understand it. "I hate cats."

Bertucci stretched, the gray map dot T-shirt rising and falling as he did so. He picked up the collage on my desk, studying the photos, the ticket stubs I'd taped to posterboard, our original nametags. Codman's said, "Hi! My name's Jane." Bertucci's said, "Hi! My name's not Steve. Can you guess what it is?" Mine said, "Hi! My name's Olivia but you may call me Frederica for short."

Bertucci picked at his tag. "This is so old."

"Don't ruin that!" I said. And then I read aloud a fun fact from the text. "There's a rumor that when he was a lot older, Schrödinger actually told an audience that he wished he'd never met the cat."

Bertucci didn't answer and his eyes were kind of blank when he turned to look at me. And while I suspected Codman was breaking up with Lissa right then and that's why he wasn't at my house listening to the cat's peculiar fate, I couldn't be sure. I couldn't see in the box, right?

◦ ◦ ◦ ◦

One song ended, the few seconds of quiet bouncing off the Circle's concrete walls. Then another song started, this one unfamiliar. I was paused there, with Schrödinger and my bag, debating leaving or staying, feeling stuck in between.

I listened to the words. *Meet me in the middle of the night.* Okay, done. I listened more. The song was upbeat, catchy; had I heard it before? Yes. No. I put my face in my hands, trying to free up my mind enough to recall when. Bertucci's whistle. Whistling. The night of *The Rashomon Effect*? No. Marta's there. The main theater.

I picked Schrödinger up, and when he wriggled too much, I set him down. He took off behind the ticket booth and I chased him, bashing my already hurt shin on the ticket box that probably held bits and pieces of all the movies I'd seen. I couldn't let the cat just run away and be stuck in the Circle forever, so I grabbed it. In my arms, Schrödinger seemed to settle.

I slid my pack around front, unzipped the main compartment, and set Schrödinger in there. He mewed at me. "I'm zipping you in there," I assured him. I zipped the sides but not the top, and he peeked his head and front paws over as I slung the backpack on.

The main theater! I could see it—the anti-Oscars. Bertucci whistling this tune incessantly. Me asking him to stop. "Romeo's Tune," it's called. "All you need is a good speech and a balcony," he'd said.

I gripped the backpack and sprinted, running as though being chased, desperate to get to the main theater, to the balcony, panicked that I would get there too late, that I would arrive to find Bertucci's body pitched over the side, lifeless and on the floor, his gray T-shirt making sure I knew *you are here.*

I tripped and stumbled, pulled myself back up without thinking, ditching the lobby and the exit doors in a frantic attempt to beat the clock.

I got to the balcony to find I was not alone.

"You showed up," Codman said.

"No, you showed up. This time." I paused. "Or, you know, you didn't just leave me to fend for myself."

We stood there, not looking over the balcony's edge, not talking while I caught my breath. His green eyes locked onto mine as my chest pounded.

"Can I just tell you something and not have you make fun of me?" I asked, the words slight as I tried to make my breath even.

"Sure." Codman looked out of breath too, though he hadn't been running or at least hadn't been on the stairs when I had. The music kept going, the cheery tune antithetical to the mood.

"'Bring me stolen kisses from your room, '" I said. "Did you hear that? That line?" Codman nodded. It was possible he knew the songs as well as I did, or that he'd heard Bertucci whistle the tune.

"Is that what you wanted to say?" Codman asked me.

"No." I gripped the edge of the balcony, fighting the urge to look over, to see the view, the height, what lay beneath. "Don't laugh. God, I hope you don't think I'm totally bonkers." I took a shaky breath. "Codman, I'm petrified. Afraid to look down because . . . because I'm worried I'm going to find Bertucci's body down there."

Codman looked at me, came closer, put his hands out to touch me but then drew them back and into his pockets. "Oh my God, me too," he admitted. "I mean, we won't. We won't."

He took a step toward the edge, pressing his body into the balcony. I could see his legs shaking.

Slowly, so slowly, we peered over the edge. I could see it, the outline, splayed like a chalk body on the sidewalk, blood seeping into the time-worn carpet.

"Of course not," I sighed. "Of course there's nothing."

Codman

Of course there wasn't. Only, I couldn't shake that feeling.

Olivia and I were wired after that, glad and scared and relieved all at once, and then, right in the midst of all of those feelings, a light flickered on the screen in front of us. The heavy curtain was drawn to the side, and a film started up.

Blurred trees, first in spring, the green electric, the magnolias unfurled. Bertucci's view from the train, crossing the tracks from his side of town to the college campus. Spring merged into summer shots, the view of a baseball field with a large expanse of grass behind it.

"Is that the one near here?" I asked. Livvy nodded.

"He must have filmed this on his way to classes. Look—see the field was empty, then filled with Canada geese. Then baseball. Now..."

"Bikinis. God love Bertucci." The film paused, focused, zoomed in on a particular sunbather. White bikini, breasts spilling out just enough. Lissa.

"Nice." Olivia sounded wounded. I reached for her arm, but she pulled it away.

Then the camera backed way up, unfocused, zoomed in again on another body, this one clothed. Olivia. Knees bent to her chest as she sat under a shaded tree with a book. She looked not at Lissa but at me, also on the grass, looking at Lissa.

"We had a picnic that day," I said, and it was nearly a whisper. "I tried telling her the story and all I could . . . she didn't respond how I wanted."

"Yeah, well, you can't control everything, can you?" Livvy asked, her eyes forward, afraid to look at me.

"No, the thing is she couldn't respond right because she wasn't . . . she isn't you. I kept waiting for you."

Olivia groaned. "*You* wait for *me*? Give me a break. After everything that's happened? I've spent years wai—" She cut herself off, and the images kept coming.

On screen, Olivia sat reading, her mouth moving but I couldn't hear the words. She sat on a bed that wasn't hers, perched on the edge.

"Bertucci's mom," she said. Olivia leaned forward as though magically the screen might show more, get wider, reveal the unseen. "She liked me to read to her. Bertucci listened sometimes. But I think it was hard too. For him to listen. Oh—look—there you are."

I had come in one Monday when I knew Bertucci was at the hospital and picked up bottles from the back porch. They were lined up and nicely organized, which struck me as pathetic though it made for easier loading into the cardboard boxes I'd brought.

"He wasn't there. He was at the hospital." My voice came out insisting this, though obviously it wasn't true. "Why?"

"He saw everything we did for him, I guess. Maybe he wants us to know that he knows."

"What?" I felt the blood drain from my face. "Say that again."

"He knows."

"*I know. I know.* That's what he knows!" I flailed my hands. "Right."

"What?" Olivia frowned, confused.

"Don't worry about it," I said as more footage came on the screen. The outside of the hospital, a focus on the Emergency Entrance sign. Filmed only from the outside. He hadn't gone in. Then a shot of all of our shoes, discarded by the edge of the community pool. That part I'd seen him film. He'd said how reassuring it was, seeing the pairs of shoes together. How when he saw one shoe on the side of the road, all he could think was, where's the other one? What had happened? Something tragic, Bertucci said. Olivia, gazing out the window of Bertucci's bedroom, watching us play one-legged Frisbee like wobbly flamingos, painfully off-kilter but laughing.

"How did he manage to be in two places at once?" I asked.

Olivia shook her head, then sat up very straight. "Remember? The best directors capture what no one is supposed to see."

I swallowed hard. *The Rashomon Effect.* "Did you find the tiny theater?" I asked. Olivia nodded.

"The impartial viewer," Olivia said.

"He's not impartial! Bertucci—you are not impartial!" I yelled, and Olivia shot me a look that made me shut up.

"If he had a camera set up in his room—let's assume he had this much of the time if not all," Olivia said. She looked scared again, glanced quickly over the balcony then back at me. "Do you think he saw . . ."

I considered her. Not just the situation but everything that was Olivia Reinstein. Her long e-mails from exotic places. Her ability to find the subtext in everything I said. Her jealousy of Lissa's place in the high school hierarchy or her relationship with me. How Livvy looked beautiful when she was sad and how it killed me to see her that way. How I didn't have to explain myself, and how she actually enjoyed having dinner with my parents even if they picked at her emotional state the way they used chopsticks—that is, skillfully and not entirely without motive. How she was more than competence porn and actually the best of everything.

"You mean do I think Bertucci knew that we kissed?" I asked. Olivia nodded. "Did he have to see to know?"

"Schrödinger's Cat," Olivia said.

"Blah-blah-blah huh?" I asked.

"I have a cat in my backpack, just so you know." She motioned to it with her chin.

I looked at her with doubt. "A live cat? You hate cats."

"It's a long story," she said. "It involves quantum physics."

The film flickered; crackling white spots appeared on the screen.

A final shot of a beach, the sand half water-darkened and half light, rocks spelling out our names, Livvy then mine then B-E-R-T-U- cut off by the rising tide as though he intended it to get washed away.

"The beach house. That day? Lakeville? Your disgusting theory of murders there?" Livvy looked scared, regretful.

"He had sand on his hands when he had that tuna sandwich," I nodded. "We stayed at the house."

The reel ended and flashes of white brilliance darted across the screen.

We sat there in crackled silence with the cat meowing, when something hit me.

"Something's wrong." I looked at her and saw my own fear mirrored back to me. "Didn't he say something about that once?" I tried to remember, my lungs filling fast now, my pulse quickening. "Film can catch fire. Weren't you there when he gave me that lecture? With that story about some movie house back in the thirties and how all these people perished and—"

Though she said she hadn't been there to hear that story, we both bolted from the balcony back toward the projector room, the urgency building all around us. It was easy to imagine—us burning to death in a romantic and tragic end, the balcony in its entirety crumbling under the weight of the flames, the whole building razed with only charred remains left for someone to find.

Livvy

We got there in what felt like the nick of time. I unbuckled the reel from the projector and tried to hold it but it was heavier than I thought, unwieldy. It fell out of my hands and onto the floor with a crash. Codman crouched to pick it up and I met him on the floor, my pack sliding off, the cat still there, peeking out at the whole scene.

The room wasn't dark exactly, but faded, like it couldn't get light but wasn't ready to wilt completely. On the wooden shelves all around us, old filmstrips dangled from their reels, blowing ghostly in a slight breeze.

Codman knelt by me, his hands on the reel, the reel of us and everything we'd been, up until now.

I looked at him, and he set the reel down.

He moved in toward me, and I moved forward, closing the gap between us. His mouth looked ready, and his eyes went from mine to my lips and then back to my eyes. He put one hand on the back of my head, the other gently on my neck.

"Why haven't we ever been able to be together? Really be together?" I asked when he was only inches away. That weekend at the beach I'd had high hopes—we'd played Scrabble late into the night, the waves splashing outside, the air tinged with expectation.

How many of my memories were of the three of us? We overlapped like rope twists, unable to be untangled. Rumors had started, faded, started again about the three of us being too close, about me dating them both, about them dating each other. "It was always the three of us," I said.

"And that's why." Codman's hands were solid and light on my skin, his fingertips electrifying and comforting all at once.

"Yeah," I said, "but I can't help thinking that . . . tonight . . . now? That we're supposed to—"

"That the plan is *us*?" He drew an invisible line back and forth between his chest and mine and then put his hands right back onto me.

I nodded. "Is that what you think?"

Codman's breath was shaky. "Olivia."

"Livvy."

"Livvy—you're . . . I know I am the sad-sack son of people who talk about feelings for a living and that of anyone, I should be able to tell you how I feel. But . . . I'm not some sort of film montage genius. I can't write poems or equations." He whispered into my ear, making my hair stand up, my already-racing heart pound. "But I can't leave here without knowing we're together."

I nodded into him. "Together together?"

"Yes yes," he said and I semi-laughed. "You can repeat it however many times you want, but the truth is that we should be together and everyone knows it. And I'm sorry I left you."

I leaned in to kiss him, and we were close enough that I could feel his lips but not firmly. I backed up slightly. "What if Bertucci walked in now?"

Codman flinched. "He won't."

"But if he did," I said.

Codman let go of me. The absence I felt without his hands stung me and I was cold, shaking. He took a deep breath and tried one more time, sweeping his arm around my waist and right as the kiss was about to happen, we could see him.

Bertucci.

"Bertucci," I whispered.

Codman nodded.

He had interrupted us and I hated him for that, but what I hated him for wasn't only that. "I hate this," I said. And then, unable to fight it any longer, I began to cry. I missed Bertucci so much it clawed at me.

"I know," Codman said, his green eyes fighting it too.

Bertucci said nothing.

He would never say anything.

Not another word.

Whether I could see in the box or not, whether I could admit the truth aloud or not, he was dead. And we'd known that for weeks.

29

Codman

It was Memorial Day. Livvy and I had gone to the Cape to her parents' house, and Bertucci had begged off. Said he wasn't feeling up to it. Ever the caretaker, Livvy had pestered him for symptoms, eager to come up with a diagnosis—strep throat, flu, chronic fatigue. She didn't want to leave him alone, but I sort of backed her into a corner. I had a feeling she wanted to go with me but that she was afraid. Worried about cutting class for the first time ever. Worried more about what could happen between us.

"Come on, you're a senior. With like three weeks until graduation. What do you care?" But she did care. She played by the rules. One of them unspoken but very real—a sort of pact we had. The three of us were the three of us. Not pairs.

But we'd taken off and left him.

. . . .

In the film projector room, the ghost of Bertucci looked at us, fading, popping up whenever I least expected it.

"Did you know he was off his meds? I don't even know when I figured out he was on anything," I asked. "I should have said more. But, I mean, to who? Bee died, and . . ."

Olivia patted the cat's head as she cried. "I did know. Or, I sort of knew. But I wasn't supposed to know. And I wasn't sure. Once when I was there with Bee, he was in the bathroom, and I thought he was looking at his mother's pills." She paused. "No. That's not true. I knew they were his. I just didn't want it to be true. I couldn't admit that he was dumping them. That he was that . . ."

We'd read this essay in English, "The White Album" with a line "we tell ourselves stories in order to live." At the time, I hadn't been that into it. But after Bertucci's funeral, when I'd ditched Olivia and the cold cuts and the stale stifling air at Bertucci's house, I'd reread it. "That's what we did, you know? We lied to ourselves. Just to get through the day with him. I mean, what would have happened if I actually called him on his crazy shit?" My hands shook. This was all the stuff I hadn't said aloud. All the stuff that piled up so huge that I felt crushed sometimes. "I talk all the time. But about nothing."

"That's not true!" Livvy insisted.

"I mean, how hard would it have been to grab him and make him take some fucking pills?"

Livvy shook her head. "He didn't want to take them anymore. That's the thing. He was done. He wasn't ever going to get better, and I think he didn't feel alive on them either."

"He was supposed to be at the hospital. That day I recycled all his father's empty bottles at his house. I did sort of have it out with him." My voice got louder as I told her. "I cornered him, you know? I was like, dude, get some fucking help. And what did I think? That he would? That I could change the outcome? No. So I get my parents involved and he's at my house all the time and I'm, like, finally able to relax for one freaking second because my parents can handle it, right? And they did. They would have. They were so good to him."

I started sobbing, which I hadn't yet. Not when we found him at his house, unmoving at the top of the stairs, and not at the funeral with his stupid shiny gold coffin, with Livvy retching in the graveyard because she had thought she was helping pick his mother's coffin but was picking Bertucci's too.

I hadn't cried then, but nothing could stop the flood now. "He said he would. Get some help, I mean. He lied."

Livvy nodded. "I don't know if you're going to think I'm crazy, but I still see him." She paused and looked around the room. "At school not so much because he just . . . wasn't there recently. But I drove by his house. And tonight—God. Tonight! He was there. Standing there, outside before we went in and . . ."

"You already had his sweater?"

She nodded. "You didn't come that night at my house. He told me about the cat and the cat was him, you know? Alive and dead at the same time. I needed you there, Alex."

"I was there. I did show up."

"You did?" She pushed her hair back from her face. "Oh, I guess so. But late. Too late.

"Hey—you called me Alex."

"That is your name, isn't it?"

"Yeah. But you always call me Codman. Why?"

She shook her head. "I don't know. I don't know half of what I do. Do you? I mean, that's the thing about Bertucci. He's . . . he was always on, always thinking. His mind was like that coaster you went on—the Big Twister. Fast, swerving, repeating, whether you asked for it or not. He was trapped."

I looked at her, the tears slipping from her cheeks to her arms. She brushed a few away with the back of her hand. "Livvy?" She looked up at me. "It's not our fault, you know.

I mean, I . . . part of me doesn't believe that yet, but I know it's true. He had this planned—the whole thing—for a long time. Probably before us."

Livvy put her head in her hands, her voice a little garbled as she spoke. "I had this stupid idea. That, even though I liked you . . . that if I'd just put my arms around him in his bathroom when I found him in there, maybe it would have changed things."

I nodded and made her look at me. "But it's not true! That's the fantasy we're telling ourselves." I rubbed my face with my hands like I was trying to wake up. "This might sound dumb, but I'll just tell you. I had a thought, too, right? That you and I . . . well . . . you and I would be together, or whatever, and Bertucci would somehow partner up with Lissa—I mean, she's fun and never mind that. The point is, it was so easy to picture it. The four of us down by Westside Park. Summer. The food truck scene picking up, and all of the laughing and going to Gordough's."

"You pictured us eating donuts?" Livvy asked.

I semi-laughed. "Maybe. It was just so real, you know?"

Livvy nodded. "I thought of things like that, too. Even with Lissa. Like in my mind I stitched together this place where he was okay."

"It's all just fantasy," I said and got the chills. "Because . . . say you're there in the bathroom, and he's thinking—well, God knows what—but you fling your gorgeous self at him and you become a couple, right? It doesn't change him. It can't affect his brain. The wiring. It's faulty."

I'd told this to my dad and he'd listened in perfect quiet, letting me churn it all up. In all of our fantasies, my dad had noted, we somehow saved him. Managed to provide such good times, such love, that he would stay.

"He stopped taking his meds."

I nodded. "He stopped his meds. Nothing we could

have done—and we did stuff, Liv. My parents couldn't help and they're trained in this. His mother couldn't help and he loved her."

"I never told mine how bad it was. My parents. I just—I knew they'd try and protect me and probably make me stay away from him just so I wouldn't be hurt or something." She took a deep, shaky breath. "After we . . . after you and I found him, I told them, obviously."

I sighed. "He was so perfect at planning."

"Except for that." Livvy took my hand, and I remembered showing up at his house, barefoot from the beach.

The night before had been pretty much perfect. Scrabble, pizza, Livvy and I had the house all to ourselves with the double bed in the front room. We'd gone to the beach, stripped down, waded into the water that was cold, too cold to stay in, and maybe I'd only gone in so I'd have an excuse to warm up in the outside shower. Which we had. And when I'd seen Livvy, her face clear in the slanted moonlight, I knew I loved her. I'd told her and we'd gone upstairs, slipped into the clean sheets and spent the whole night together.

First thing in the morning, she'd woken me. The sun wasn't even up, just rays of pink streaking the horizon.

"We have to tell him," she'd said, and I knew I wouldn't convince her to stay the rest of the weekend. Mainly because I knew she was right. You couldn't delay the inevitable.

We couldn't let Bertucci slip away from us like that. Couldn't keep the truth from him. There we were building a new future together—the whole summer and everything after, possibly together without him.

So we'd gathered all our crap and climbed into the car, laughing and exhilarated, stopping only at Dunkin' Donuts for coffee and Munchkins, licking powdered sugar from each other's fingers as we drove away from the beach and back to town.

"We'll just surprise him," Livvy had said. The sunlight crackled on the car's exterior, burning my hand as I let my palm rest out the window.

"We'll tell him we thought he should have been there with us," I said.

Livvy slowed the car outside Bertucci's, the tires popping on the random bits of gravel on the scrubby driveway. "We can't say that," she'd said. "Because it's not really true anymore, is it?"

I tried to picture Scrabble with Bertucci. He would have won, of course, and liked the fact that I'd played "ukulele," but he wouldn't have let us swim or shower or share a bed. "No. I guess you're right." I sighed and squeezed her hand. "But it's hard, you know? Telling him. Like the end of something."

We'd parked and, like so many times before, gone around to the porch with its ripped screens and discarded folding tables, the withering houseplants and multiple cardboard boxes all filled with more bottles.

＊ ＊ ＊ ＊

"The house was so, so still," I said to Livvy, and she nodded, remembering. The door squeaked. It was sunny and quiet and empty in the kitchen. "What if," I said, "we hadn't come back then?"

Livvy digested those words. "I have repeated that so many times—that question. I don't think it matters. I mean, he'd still be dead. We'd be saved that image of him, I guess. He just got his timing wrong—he thought we'd stay there, that his dad would find him probably."

In a fit of honesty, we had braced ourselves and dashed up the stairs, past the photos of kid Bertucci on the walls, taken back before any of this was happening maybe, and burst through the door hoping to surprise him, to rattle the unflinching master of planning. "When I see him, and I do . . . I mean, a vision of him . . . he's still wearing that shirt."

Livvy nodded. "You are here."

"We are here." I stopped. "All night I saw him too. Outside, I swear I could see his creepy eyes. How he'd want Twizzlers and make silly comments in the art gallery. Do you think I'm nuts for talking to him?" I looked at her. "Out loud. I mean, I talk to him out loud, Liv." I took a breath. "I'm serious when I say I saw him here. Not just talked to him but really, I can, like, conjure him up."

"Me too." She chewed her lip for a minute. "I see him all over the place, his actual mannerisms. I fill the conversation with what he'd say." She pushed her hair out of her face. "I think we will. Or, I will, for a while. Maybe always. I don't know." She held out her phone. "I still text him."

"I know you do."

"The thing is, I know he'll never read them—he probably wouldn't have even when he was . . . alive. But it feels better to me." She palmed the phone like it was Bertucci's unmoving hand.

"I owed him eight hours," I told her. "When you were in Morocco, buying those death masks?" Livvy shuddered. "We were bored. I planned this fun day. Or, I thought it was fun, visiting all the tollbooths in the New England area."

"Why is that fun?" Livvy asked.

I shook my head. "It wasn't. I think . . . maybe I was trying to make things normal. For Bertucci. Like the Day of the Meters."

"Night of 1,000 Escalators?" Livvy licked her lips. "The thing is, it wasn't normal. It was . . . those were all signs."

"I know. I know. Of mental illness. Believe me, I've been over this fifty times with my dad. But anyway, the tollbooth thing was expensive—the Pike is like five bucks. And it was lame. Eight hours of driving around, and I forgot to bring the mix I'd made—with money songs on it, of course."

"And?"

"And when we got back, Bertucci got out of the car and leaned in the window and looked at me in that way he has—had."

Livvy knew what I meant. "This look? The kind but glaring look?" She demonstrated. I nodded.

"All he said was, 'You owe me these past eight hours back.'"

Livvy reached for my hand and I squeezed hers. "I think you paid him back," she said. And then, because I could tell it wasn't really what she wanted to say, she added, "It wasn't your fault."

Livvy

We stayed in the projector room for what felt like a very long time, so long that by the time we emerged, making our way from the main theater out to the lobby, the light had shifted. Early morning. The same time of day we'd left the beach and returned—unexpectedly—to Brookville.

Codman went over to the ticket booth and picked up a large painting. "Bob," he explained. I loved that he only had to say one word and yet there was a whole story in there. That even without Bertucci, the story existed.

The cat meowed, and I realized that I now had a pet for the first time. And that Codman had a painting he'd take with him to college or wherever he wound up. What a weird collection of things we had.

Codman cleared his throat. "I just—I need you to know that even though Bertucci was the planner . . . I had ideas, too. Not like his. But . . ." He held the painting of Bob against his leg and I knew—knew with absolute certainty—that Bertucci would manage to send postcards—via Bob—from the grave. They might not arrive right away, but I had a feeling they'd show up.

I shifted my pack around to get a look at Schrödinger and, once I'd confirmed he was okay, slid the pack back. "You shouldn't have left me at Bertucci's," I said. "Not just because his dad was wasted and his aunt was screaming. But . . . I mean, my parents stayed. You should have stayed."

"I know." Codman's face was lined with sorrow, his mouth turned down into a quivering frown. "Not that I'm trying to make excuses or anything. . . . I just want you to know." He took a deep breath, preparing. "One time, I went over to pick you up. I don't know—we were meeting at Bertucci's." Codman shook his head. "He was studying and fairly calm at the time—I understand now, he was medicated—and anyway, I had this thought: what if we—just me and you, Livvy—drove off together. Anywhere."

I looked at him and felt nervousness—not just the same shakiness I'd had since finding Bertucci but the one I'd experienced the night before, at the beach house. A good nervous.

Codman continued, "Anyway, you came out of the doorway, and I was nervous so I looked down, and all I had on me—all I had in the car—was two drumsticks, a fork leftover from a salad I ate watching that tennis match against Brookville West, a jawbreaker, and a condom." He paused. "Not that I had any hope in hell of using it at that point."

"What are you trying to say?"

"I don't know." He paused. "No. Wait. I do know! You and I didn't run off together. In fact, you might remember I didn't even suggest it; instead I think I bored the crap out of you with my stories of camping as a kid. But . . . what I'm trying to say is that I know now I couldn't have done it then. Run off with you. It had to happen the way it did."

I nodded. "And it did. Happen, you know?"

He'd left me there in the dirty sunlight of Bertucci's kitchen, cups of Diet Coke and lukewarm beers near the sink. But he'd also left me after what we'd done the night before.

Codman came close to me, carrying his painting as though he were worried about leaving it behind. "Livvy. I do not. For one second. Regret anything that happened on the beach or with you."

"Even though it was sort of the precursor to everything else?" I asked.

"I think that's the thing. You and I have to figure out how to . . . not skip over that, because we can't. But sort of have it be two stories. There's the story where you and I are at the beach and falling in love—" He looked at me for a sign of approval, and I gave it with a smile. "And then another story, right?"

"The one where we're too honest for our own good and come back too early and find what we're not supposed to." I nodded.

Outside, the city was waking up. Inside, so were we.

"Ready?" Codman walked toward the side door. "Hey—the Slice delivered?"

"Yeah—two calzones." I paused. Two grads. Not three. "I ate mine without you. Sorry. It's probably cold now."

"Like that ever stopped me?" Codman said and unwrapped the tinfoil, holding the calzone in a football grip. He ate it quickly.

I held open the door, the same one we'd broken into the night before, though it felt like longer, as though it had happened to someone else a long time ago. "You coming?"

Codman nodded, wiped his mouth on a waxy white napkin, and threw the food into a trash bin.

I opened the door and something landed on my head. Should I have known better than to look up? Probably. By now, yes. But I looked up and so did Codman and we were pelted; chocolate-covered raisins, Junior Mints, gummy bears, all manner of tiny edibles—stale and thus even harder than normal—rained down on my face, sliding down the back of my shirt.

"A gummy bear just landed between my breasts!" I tried to duck and dodge the storm of sweets, but I couldn't.

"Oh, to be a tiny, chewy bear," Codman said. I kicked him lightly. "What? I gotta be me. Where'd he get all this?" He paused. "I mean, it was Bertucci, right? All of it?"

"He rigged it to spill only on leaving." I pointed up to the twine and bucket. I nodded. Then I put another piece together. "The dead snack bar. The boxes were all empty."

"So he gathered them?"

I plucked a green Jujube from Codman's head. "It's . . . I don't know . . . it's sad to picture him."

I could see it, Bertucci methodically undoing each box of candy, dumping the contents into a bucket, and then carefully sealing the boxes back up as though nothing had been removed. Even though I'd stopped crying before, I felt it well up again and realized I might have more tears, more images that would filter in. Not just today or this week, but all summer, next year, as an adult even. That in order to get the memories back the way they actually happened, I would have to let all sadness come in and wash out. Then I would be able to look back on the Day of the Meters or Memorial Day with a smile maybe, not regret and melancholy.

"You know that nostalgia literally means pain from an old wound?" I said, thinking how Bertucci would have said he knew that already. And he would have liked that I knew it and felt he was a little better than Codman because he didn't.

Codman started laughing and, in the laughing, tearing up. "I mean, it's kind of hysterical, really. Bertucci sitting with a cat, probably feeding it all this time and dealing with eighty pounds of stale candy, calling the Slice five months in advance . . . and a fake skull." He paused. "Oh, shit, where's my skull?" I pointed to his head. "Ha, ha. Thanks, Anatomy Girl. No, I mean my little blue skull. It kind of got me through the freakazoid nature of my night."

"He was really good at it," I said.

"At what? Making candy rain on us?"

"No. The grand gesture."

Codman nodded, tried eating a piece, and spat it out on the floor. "Anyone can make some big gesture. All dramatic and showy. The question is—and I thought about this while we weren't . . . when you and I weren't . . ."

"When we weren't speaking. It's okay. We are now. Just go on."

"Well, Bertucci kicked ass at all kinds of stuff, right? But remember when he helped that guy Matthew with the prom dilemma?"

Everyone at Brookville fell prey to the pressurized spring tradition of the grand prom gesture—asking people in creative ways, each one cooler than the next, showstoppers with balloons in class or singing telegrams. "So, Bertucci helps Matt, right? And they cover the girl's car—the entire thing—with Post-it notes."

"It looked cool," I said. You could see them blowing in the breeze all the way from the science labs.

"Anyway, so they go through all this trouble and she says yes and they have to peel all the sticky things off the car and some of it got stuck and I remember Bertucci got roped into washing it off with some special solvent or something." Codman paused. "But he never showed."

"What do you mean?" I asked.

"Matt. He forgot to pick her up. He blew off the prom."

"And this is Bertucci's fault?" I asked.

"No. Kinda. No—more like Bertucci was so good that the idea and the execution. But he sucked at the *after*. He was all planning. Think about it—he disappeared after the hiding wall, the desk assemblage, my room on the ceiling."

I swallowed. "And us?"

"Well, I think that's what he's saying. We are the after."

I looked at the giant package of Twizzlers still unopened on the counter. "It was nice of you to put those out for him," Codman said. I nodded. "You want to take them?"

"What, and throw them into the air at graduation?" I asked. "I don't think so."

I put my hand into the doorway, stepping outside for the first time in over eight hours. The rain had left puddles that reflected the blue sky now. "Maybe you were supposed to leave the skully thing behind."

Codman opened his mouth to protest but then nodded. "Yeah, probably." Then he looked at me. "I'll be quick!" And he took off.

Even in the daylight, I felt fear, familiar and sickening, come back. He'd gone into the cinema again. With everything clear, the building itself looked precarious, disintegrating before my eyes. What if Codman never came back? I'd be stuck inside—in Schrödinger's box—forever.

I checked my watch. We had a little under two hours until we were supposed to report to the gym for cap and gown fittings and another hour in which Codman had to figure out what he was going to say in his speech to memorialize Bertucci.

He appeared next to me, emerging from the rubble panting. "Got it!" He held up the skull.

Codman

"There's something you need to see," I told Livvy. It was obvious she wanted to leave the cinema, and I did too, but I tugged her back through the lobby to the far right of the main room.

"What're you doing?" Her voice pleaded. "I just . . . we have to get out of here once and for all. . . ."

"Stop overthinking everything. For once." I put my finger on her mouth and she was quiet.

"Follow me," I said, and I hoped she would.

The door was all white, camouflaged with the wall, and I'd noticed it when I went back to retrieve the skull. "Let's just see. I think it goes to that outside staircase."

Livvy wrinkled her nose. "The creepy dilapidated wooden one?"

"Yeah, as opposed to the other finely kept features," I said.

The door opened easily, as if oiled recently, and we stepped out onto a wooden platform. The paint was peeling, and the staircase was functional if not in great shape.

"Is it possible we've had enough exploration?" Livvy

asked. She wrapped her arms around herself, and I wanted to do the same.

"Look!" I pointed to the ladder.

"Emergency exit?" Livvy asked.

I shook my head and went to test it out. "No—this must be how they changed the movie titles." The ladder was made of thin metal, flaking white in the sun, bolted to the building by rusting screws. Looking up, I could see the giant display sign.

Livvy took the rungs right after me until we were both almost all the way up to the roof. We both gripped hard onto the flimsy ladder but hung our bodies out enough to read the sign. Memories. Tears stung my eyes, and I didn't wipe them away. I was fixed on the sign until Livvy suddenly shrieked.

"Oh my God! Look!" She let go with one hand to point at the other sign, but then wobbled and nudged me forward. "Go. Go!"

I took the last rung and leaped to the roof, taking Livvy's hand after I'd landed. The black circles that had read C-I-R-C-L-E now read C-O-D-M-A-N.

"He did it," Livvy said, and for the first time she didn't look teary. She looked happy. "Your name in lights." She paused. "Of course, the lights are rusted and about to get knocked down, but . . ."

"Doesn't matter," I said. "Nothing can ruin this glory."

As I looked at the transformed letters and at Livvy, all wrinkled and beautiful in her dirty clothing and tangled hair, as I pictured speaking at graduation, I knew Bertucci was right. Only he'd seen it when I wasn't able to. I saw Livvy reach for her phone but once she'd taken it out, she didn't actually text. Instead, she took a picture and slipped it back into her pocket.

"We should head out," I said and offered Livvy my hand.

Livvy

In the parking lot, the rain had mainly dried up, but the few puddles that remained reflected the bright blue morning sky. Codman held the skull, the painting of Bob, and shook that last bits of candy out from his shirt. I took Schrödinger from my backpack, unwrapped Bertucci's sweater from my waist, and shoved it inside the bag. Would I wear it again? Yes. I would keep it and wear until it was nothing but a collection of old threads. I knew it would pain me when it finally disintegrated, but perhaps that was why I had it in the first place.

I side-stepped puddles and the cat followed, nosing the water and then padding silently next to me. My car was right where I'd left it, smack dab in the middle of the parking lot.

"Oh, shit," Codman said as he looked at the rear driveway.

I heard the siren before I turned around and saw the police car. "If I go to jail because of this, you owe me."

"I owe you? Hey, I've already worked off my hours of debt," Codman—Alex—insisted.

"Your debt to him, yeah, but what about me?" I clenched my fist as the police car slowed right near the door where we'd clipped the chains. "What about the hours I spent waiting to hear from you after your great absentia?"

"Well, I believe I've proven myself tonight. . . ." He paused. "I mean, I hope I have. But maybe we could do something else next time? Go to lunch. Collect seashells."

I smiled. "Can we?"

"Collect seashells?" he asked as the cop's siren stopped and the car door slammed. "Yes."

"Good." The night we'd spent together, Codman had picked up a single shell—not a sand dollar or anything particularly poetic but a clear, apricot-tinted one the size of my thumbnail. I'd kept it on my bedside table since, unable to pick it up or to throw it away. For the first time, I could picture accumulating more shells, collecting them with him, saving them.

"If I go to jail, take care of Bob," he said.

"And if I go, feed Schrödinger." I looked at the Circle. In the daytime, it wasn't exactly horror movie material. More just run down, ruined, and sad.

"You kids here for a reason?" the cop asked.

"Danny, you know perfectly well why we're here," Codman said, rolling his eyes at his stepbrother.

"You told him?" I asked. "All this time I'm panicked about getting caught, about my parents disowning me and spending my life in juvie or licking stamps for a living and you knew?"

Dan nodded. "I always check up on you guys. Part of the job." He hooked his thumbs through his uniform belt loops. "How'd it go, anyway?"

Codman shrugged. "Good as it could've, right Livvy?"

Livvy. He would call me Livvy now. "It was okay."

"You need a ride to graduation?" Dan asked. "I could

put the lights on, maybe speed through town?" He grinned. "Nah—you're fine. I know you'll be there. Right?"

We nodded. We watched him walk back to the cruiser, and I wondered if he'd been by in the night, if he'd checked on us or hung out in the back lot in case we'd caused trouble or something had gone wrong. He'd been the second responder after the ambulance, and maybe he felt he owed us one, too.

◦ ◦ ◦ ◦

My car was heating up from the June sun, but I put my pack on the hood and climbed up, leaning back onto the windshield. The wipers made it slightly uncomfortable, but I needed to breathe for a minute. Schrödinger leapt onto the very front of the hood and curled into a ball.

Alex climbed up next to me, leaning back into a puddle that half-soaked his shirt.

"What are you going to do with the skull?" I asked.

"I don't know." Codman held it out on his palm. The sun shone on it, making it look both toylike and gruesome. "I mean, presumably it runs out of batteries at some point, right?" But he didn't check for a slot.

"And if not?"

"I guess I just have a skull, you know?"

I nodded. We had the ugly flamingo painting taking up most of the back seat of my car, the skull in Alex's hand, a cat, and a dead friend's sweater. "It's like that song, the one at his house that time?"

"You'll have to be more specific."

"You can never leave the past behind, only accumulate more of it." I sang it and then paused. "I mean, cats live for like eighteen years or something."

"And paintings live forever."

"And I guess that's what Bertucci wanted, right?" I asked, but I didn't need Alex to answer. We'd accumulated stuff that night, but nothing compared to the mass of memories we had tucked away. We'd have to carry all of it around with us, to graduation, college, anything that lay ahead.

"Livvy? What are you doing later?" Alex asked me.

"Um, graduating, I hope. Listening to your speech. Flinging my hat up in the air."

"Cap," he said. "It's a cap. You're really going whole-hog with a movie-style fling?"

I nodded into his chest. "Why? What else is on the agenda?"

Alex cleared his throat. "Well, it's Saturday. So . . . we kind of have to feed that person's meter—if we leave the ceremony early we probably could."

I thought about it. We could carry on Bertucci's angelic meter word. "Or we could let it go."

I knew that was the real point of the night. We needed to leave it: the maze, being trapped in the darkness. I looked at Codman and, before I could edit myself, I touched his hair, his face, his real and alive self.

"Well, even if we don't feed meters, maybe we could just take a walk or something, just us?"

I nodded. "Definitely."

I could see it: the shocking new summer sun, the scar on my shin and the deeper ones inside, my sweaty fist clenching my diploma, my parents watching, how Alex Codman's parents would hug me perhaps too hard and my parents possibly not enough, and that Alex and I would kiss, hard and deep after the closing remarks. And that somehow, Bertucci would be with us.

"We should make a move," Alex said, but he didn't move yet.

"Yeah," I said, and I looked up.

I could see Codman's name up there on display for all to see. I could see the glory of what once was a state-of-the-art cinema. Maybe they'd knock it down and build useless offices or maybe a park. Urban green space that would brighten the town, or maybe the building would just stay here and rot, a sorry reminder. There was this continuous knocking down and rebuilding—malls, libraries, liquor stores. It was possible that every memory we had would be bulldozed so that we couldn't even point to any places we had all been together. Eventually, maybe every place-specific memory would disappear, a different thing in its place. Our elementary school was already rebuilt, so there'd be no way of driving by with future kids or grandkids and saying, See that? That was where we played, where we met. I looked up at the Circle's exterior billboard. "Thanks for the memories," the sign read, and I let a few tears slip down my face.

The sky was painfully blue, the sun the brightest white. Above the crumbling exterior, I could see the large gallery windows. There, inside, I could see something. It was clear. There was Bertucci, looking out at us. I couldn't make out his face, but I could see his hand. It was raised in a special wave, the same one he'd given me way back when we'd first met, only this time it wasn't hello. It was good-bye.

I lifted my own hand in response.

And then, just like that, it was time to go.

Acknowledgments

Thank you: Adam, N, S, E, and A for support, inspiration, snoozles, talks, laughs, and band names. Faye, Brendan, and Dan for reads and help early on. Kim Witherspoon, Monika Woods, and the team at Inkwell Management for soup to nuts (AKA contracts to covers). Andrew Karre for believing in the dark-weird-funny-sad and everyone at Lerner/Carolrhoda Lab. To Heather for Mahfouz, Snazbags, and the best friend and reader I could ever wish for. To JC Smith for introducing me to *Rashomon*, to the well-made play, and to Joan Didion so long ago.

This book was written as I was crawling out of the darkest time in my life. For anyone still slumping through or treading, this is also for you.

About the Author

Emily Franklin is the author of more than sixteen young adult books, including *The Half-Life of Planets* and *Tessa Masterson Will Go to Prom*, named to the 2013 Rainbow List. She is also the author of novels, short stories, and a cookbook memoir for adults. Her fiction and nonfiction have appeared on National Public Radio and in the *New York Times* and the *Boston Globe*. She lives with her husband, four kids, and enormous dog outside of Boston, Massachusetts.